TROUBLE & MALAIKA 2

Not Your Average Love Story (The Finale)

SHAYE B.

Mz. Lady P Presents, LLC

Trouble & Malaika 2

Published by Mz. Lady P Presents

www.mzladypresents.com

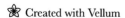

Created with Vellum

***Kendall & Kacey**, even though neither of you will read this, I mean never. Read good Christian books about staying close to Jesus. I still dedicate this to each of you for giving me a purpose. Becoming your mother gave me a reason to strive for more and to want to go out and pave a better path for each of you. I walk amongst the shadows so that both of you can bask in the light. I dedicate this to your futures; go out in the world and be great. I know that each of you will make mommy very proud!*

*To my husband, **Karl**, why you love me like you do, lol. They counted us out, but we just get stronger and stronger. No man could ever amount to you my king, my knight in camouflaged armor. I dedicate this to you for motivating me for pushing me and for never allowing me to settle for mediocrity. You've shown me parts of life that made me grow to be a better woman and a better wife. I love you endlessly. Thank you for being such a wonderful provider and greatest support.*

Acknowledgment:

To my Readers, I write to give you all a glimpse inside of my imagination. When you read my work, I want you to completely forget about everything and lose yourself in the world I have created. Forget all your problems, lay your burdens at the door and pick up one of my books and just relax. I love you all for the support and make sure you hit me up with your feedback. Thank you for reading my work and I hope that I was able to ease your troubles for a little while. Until next time, BE GREAT & LET THAT ASS SHAKE (I know I'm lame just roll with it though).

To my lovely pen sisters and pen brother, it's an honor to be amongst so many dope authors. All of you are simply amazing!

To my pen sis, **AJ Davidson**, you know you my bihhhh! Thanks, for always responding when I blow you up 24/7. You're always there to help me and to give me honest feedback and a listening ear. You are becoming a very close friend, and I love you sis.

To **Keitha Chatman**, thank you for being an amazing test reader and for always supporting my work as well as my pen sisters.

Last but certainly not least, to Mz. Lady P, thank you for seeing potential in me. I still remember freaking out after receiving the email from you. I was like no way one of my favorite authors liked my work. I'm so grateful and ready to put in this work to make you proud. I'm repping MLPP proudly.

Keep Up With Shaye B

FACEBOOK: AUTHOR SHAYEB

FACEBOOK LIKE PAGE: Shaye B.
FACEBOOK READING GROUP: Shaye B's Urban Lit Trap House
IG: authorshayeb
TWITTER: authorshayeb

Synopsis

Fame thought he made the right choice by letting Shanty go, but he never imagined that she would give her heart to another man. After Shanty ignored his warning, he was forced to hold up to his promise. What was supposed to be a happy ending for Shanty and Neron turned a huge disaster with Shanty getting caught in the crossfire. Has Fame's hot-headed ways finally caught up to him? It's a hard pill to swallow watching the woman you love, give her all to another man.

Ice and Niyah were on cloud nine this second chance around. Things were so perfect that something was bound to go wrong. Ice found out that his perfect woman was yet another snake. Torn between trusting in his heart and protecting his empire Ice makes a decision that no one sees coming, dragging out a mountain of skeletons and secrets in the process. What was the real reason behind Niyah betraying the love of her life?

Trouble & Malaika left off stronger than ever in part one. Trouble finally let his guard down, admitting that he needs her. They fight to become the person that the other needs but in the end, they are left contemplating if their troubling love is even worth it.

We pick up right where we left off, and things take explosive twists and turns for the Trouble & Malaika gang. The past and the present mesh when the couples bump heads. Will this be a case of makeups to breakups or a series of the one that got away? Tune in to find out.

Previously...

Shanty

"I don't know y'all! Maybe I should just call it off; we don't have to have this big ass ceremony," I said, walking back and forth. I was sweating out my fucking makeup. I know I was wetting my dress up at the armpits.

"Bitch, pull it to-fucking-gether. OK! You got me to dye my fucking hair black for this shit oh bitch yo ass is getting fucking married. If I gotta drag you down that fucking aisle!" Niyah snapped, and Lai gave her a look.

"Listen Shanty. I think this is about more than Fame threatening to shoot up the church. So right now, before Neron's mother and family waltz in here, tell us what's up," Lai said, and I sighed.

"What if this is a mistake. Fame is all I know and deep in my heart I know I will always love him. I feel like I'm betraying him, but I don't think I can go on waiting forever for him to get his shit together, either," I felt tears threatening. I still love Fame with all my heart, but Neron is so fucking amazing, and I know that he will be devoted to me. We have something good, but deep down I wish it were Fame sometimes.

"Oh, no bitch, I'm about to give you the same advice somebody needs to give Tisha Campbell-Martin on her singing career. Are you ready," Niyah said, looking at me seriously, and I nodded.

"LET IT THE FUCK GO! QUIT! STOP! TAKE THAT SHIT AND THROW IT THE FUCK AWAY!" she screamed, and Lai turned her head to try to act like she wasn't laughing, but I could hear her giggling.

"No but seriously, you gave that nigga too many damn years to get it right, and he still fucked up. Don't you miss out on your good thing holding on to a hope, a wish, and a dream that ain't ever coming. Don't set yourself up like that. You deserve to be happy, shit. You ain't stared my ass down in months and bitch we stayed in a stare down every other Saturday," I laughed and smiled genuinely.

"Ice is changing this bitch," I said, looking at Lai, and she gave me a cosigning finger point. "I just wish Mama Rosemary was coming," I added, and Lai smiled.

"Who said she wasn't?" Lai asked, and I started looking around for my mama. Lai went over to the door and opened it up, and my mama waltzed in looking like she was fresh off the runway. Mama Rosemary was 45 and looked like she was every bit of 25. She stood at 5'6 with smooth chocolate skin and slant cat eyes that had a youthful charm to them. Long kinky curls fell to her back, and her body was snatched! Mama works out faithfully. She looks absolutely gorgeous in her white jumpsuit. The arms of it draped down and around like a cape. She looked like she was a queen ready to take her throne.

"Mama!" I cried rushing to her, and she pulled me close.

"Cut that out before you mess up your pretty makeup" she fussed, but I cried harder. I thought she wasn't coming because Fame was against it.

"You came," I cried, and she looked at me like I was crazy.

"I was just picking up the damn dress with you, Shanty. Now, why would I help you plan a damn wedding I wasn't coming to. I don't pay Tyrell any mind, and you shouldn't either. Ian missing no weddings, birthdays, births, or nothing else for none of y'all. Now pull yourself together before them bougie ass people come on up in here. You know that they're mad as hell you ain't signed a prenup," we all laughed at her.

"I think we all need a shot and a twerk session. Mama Rosemary's too cute, and she's got all that big ole country ass sitting right in that jumpsuit, AYEEEE!!!" Niyah yelled, hyping us all up.

"We are in a church for Christ sakes," Neron's mother, Nuru, said and we all rolled out eyes. "Good heavens what happened to your makeup dear, and you are sweating profusely. This is precisely why I had the designer create two gowns. Oh, no, no, no. This will not do. Eliana! Get the stylist in here. Come now, Shantalya. We must get you out of this gown and into the other one this minute." She rushed me, and I went along with it. Forty-five minutes later, I was dressed, my makeup was redone, and I loved this outcome.

My dress is a long-sleeved trumpet gown with sheer lace sleeves and Swarovski crystals all over. The back is very low cut but still modest; I just love the way it hugs my body and accentuates my thick curves. My train was damn near a mile long. Nuru walked over with a sheer lace cape lined in crystals, and my jaw dropped. It was just as long if not longer than my train. She snapped it around the front of my neck, and the crystals sat at my neckline like a dazzling necklace.

"Okay, okay, it's time for the favors," Mama Rosemary said, walking up to me. "This is the something old," she handed me a beaded bracelet. It was old and dirty, but I remember it perfectly. It was the something I made in class for Mother's Day. It was my first one with her.

"This was the best gift you ever gave to me. Don't yo ass go and lose my shit; I want it right back," I laughed because she was trying to talk big to keep from crying.

"I have something blue for you," Lai said, handing me her favorite guitar pick.

I knew it meant a lot for her to give me that cause Lai doesn't hold on to anything. I had to fight to get her to buy her bridesmaids dress so bad that Trouble ended up buying it. She refuses to touch her inheritance if it's not for daily needs.

"Okay move Lai I need my turn before everything starts up!"

Niyah loud mouth ass yelled, pushing Lai who pushed her right back.

"My arm still hurts from the bullet, but I can still fight. Don't try me, Niyah!" Lai spat, and we laughed cause she was dead serious, and Niyah knew better than to mess with her again.

"I got the new and the borrowed," Niyah said, popping the band on a stack and making it rain on me. I started to do a little dance, catching a bill and stuffing it in my dress.

"Enough of all of that let's get this ceremony started," the wedding planner said, handing me my bouquet. She sounds just like Neron's stuck up mother right about now.

Everyone lined up to exit, but the TV scene popped on and Neron's handsome face flashed across the screen. He was smiling so damn bright that it took all my doubts away. I have fallen so hard for this man.

"I love you," he mouthed, and I bucked my eyes, realizing that he could see me.

"NO! THIS IS BAD LUCK!" I shouted, trying to hide, but he just shrugged it off.

"Nothing can stop what's already in motion. Come down that aisle to me love," he said, blowing a kiss before the screen went back black.

As we line up, I was standing back waiting for my moment to walk down to my man. I could hear Lai singing some bullshit Neron's mother told her to sing, but the moment was so special that I wasn't even mad at it.

My time came, and I was shocked when Neron walked down the aisle to get me. My brothers are all being assholes ditching my wedding, so I was stuck walking down by myself.

"Don't sweat what we can't change, love. From this day forth we walk every path together," he said, kissing my cheek.

Shaking off the emotion, I tucked my arm in his. I was overwhelmed with emotion as we walked down the aisle. Neron's mother basically took over, and I'm happy she did. Everything looks so amazing, just simply and elegant. Our colors are classic black and white. The bridesmaid's dresses are short white flowy gowns with sweetheart necklines. I only had Lai and Niyah, so Neron's family filled the rest of the spots. When we made it down the aisle, Mama Rosemary stood to give me away formally, and I kissed her cheek.

Neron and I took our places and before the damn preacher could get his words out the door burst back open. I look down, and Fame had a whole gang of fine niggas with him, Ice, and Trouble. Fame took my breath away with his sexy ass. I was tempted to run into his arms.

"Bitch!!! Them some fine ass niggas GAH DAMN!" one of Neron's sisters said.

I was so caught up in staring at how handsome Fame looked that I didn't even pay attention to the guns. I was busy fighting temptations to push Neron aside and tell Fame to take his place. One cue they all lifted their guns and started shooting the ceiling and walls. Fame was the exception; his gun was pointed right for Neron and me. It was like everything was moving in slow motion when I saw the flash from the muzzle of the gun. Something hot pierced through my flesh, and I went flying backward.

ONE

Shanty

"That crazy bastard shot up my fucking wedding!" I cried as the doctor was trying his best to work on me.

"Shanty, calm the hell down. You more worried about that wedding, getting shot!" Mama shouted, grabbing me by the face.

I'm so damn mad that I don't know what to do. Neron is pacing around the room on the phone, holding an ice pack to his eye. My whole wedding was fucked up thanks to the ignorant son of a bitch. I swear everything I had in me for that nigga left when he pointed that gun at me and pulled the fucking trigger. That shit hit me so damn hard that I flew back like a cheap wig in a windstorm. A bitch ain't know what the fuck hit me.

From there all hell broke out. Neron and his brothers charged Fame and our brothers. Shit ended bad, especially since Neron and nem got their asses whooped. A bitch was laying there half-dead, and them stupid ass nigga was too busy fighting to even check my damn pulse. Thank God for my mama, Lai, and Niyah. Without them, I might have been dead. Lai held pressure to my wound while mama talked to me keeping my conscious. At the time, I thought that nigga shot me in the chest cause I could barely fucking breathe. My whole life hurt.

"Mama, the doctor just said my shoulder will be fine. So, it's safe for me to be mad about my wedding right now. Fame went too far this time. I don't even want nothing to do with him period. He is dead to me; this is unforgivable. Trouble and Ice are walking the tightrope; they were dead wrong," I fumed, staring into her eyes.

I could tell she was upset still from seeing me on the ground bleeding like that. The whole time she was praying and begging me to stay awake while screaming for Niyah to hurry up, but that bitch never came back after going to call the ambulance.

"Anybody found Niyah yet?" I asked, looking at Lai who shook her head no.

"We were so busy getting you here that we didn't even notice. I'll call Trouble to see if he can get a hold of her," Lai said, walking out to go find a pay phone. Me nor Mama have our phones with us here.

I finally sat back allowing the doctor to nurse my wound. The bullet went through and through, missing anything major. My ass landed on the communion, fracturing a rib. That's what had me breathing so heavy. The doctor said that the bullet only tore ligaments in my shoulder, it missed the bone completely. I will need plenty physical therapy, but I will be fine in some months. The pain will be persistent through it all though. If I weren't doped up on them pain pills, I'd be doubled over right now.

All in all, I'm lucky as fuck because people have died from gunshot wounds to the shoulder. Allowing myself to relax, I looked over at my husband. I hated seeing him this way. He looks so devastated. He hasn't said a word to me since the shit happened. He's just been on that phone calling around trying to use his connections to get some justice. I don't have the heart to tell him that the people Fame was with can do whatever the hell they want in these streets and nobody will check them. They're too connected.

"Well make it right, Trevor! That's what I pay you for!" he barked, throwing his phone against the wall rushing out of the room.

I've never seen him this mad before; I instantly felt bad because it's all my fault. I should have told Neron about Fame's threat, but I wasn't paying Fame no mind at the time. I really thought he was just trying to scare me into doing what he wanted. Tears poured down my face, and I just let them because I couldn't move my arm.

"It's okay, baby. He's just stressed out. Hell, wouldn't you be if your fiancé got shot at you wedding; and then you turn around and get yo ass beat down?" Mama asked, and I tried my best not to laugh at her ass but I couldn't.

"He's my husband, Ma," I corrected.

"Baby, I know they got you flying high on that good shit, but Fame shot up the wedding before he could even lift the veil," she said, making me laugh harder.

"We got married two weeks ago. The wedding was just a formality because Neron wanted give me the fairytale experience," I said, and she cocked her head, putting her hand on her hip.

"Lord, where the hell is my back scratcher when I need it!" she fussed, biting her bottom lip popping me. The doctor gave her a look, and she cocked her head rolling her neck daring him to say something. He held his hands up in surrender before finishing patching me up.

"Like I was finna say. How the hell you go and get married without telling me?"

"Cause you can't hold water, Rosemary," I said, and she popped me again. I was so damn numb ian feel shit.

"You damn right! I was gone call up everybody to come see my baby girl land her a whale. If I ain't done nothing right I taught you that!" she said, causing me to shake my head. Before I could even respond, Lai walked back into the room.

"Trouble says Niyah is with Ice. I've been trying to call her, but her phone is going to voicemail. I think it's because it's an unknown number. I'm going to call her back once I get home later with Trouble's phone," she said.

The doctor was done patching me up, and he gave me something stronger than the pain medication I was on. At the same time, Neron walked back in grabbing my hand. With a passionate kiss, he looked me in my eyes, placing his forehead against mine.

"Love, I'm sorry this happened, but know that I will never let anything happen to you again. Please forgive me for failing to protect you," he sounded so damn sad it broke my heart.

"It's not your fault, baby," I whisper, kissing his lips. I was trying my best to stay coherent, but the meds were taking me under.

"I'll give you a better wedding love, and I'll give you a better life than anything you could dream of," I heard him say before the meds took over; I was out in seconds.

TWO

Fame

"Nigga, you fucking shot her!" Trouble shouted, pushing me. Yir and Ju held him back as I leaned my head back against the wall.

"I fucked up, Troub," I said, feeling myself getting worked up like a bitch.

"Aye, fam we gone head out and give y'all some time. Be easy on him, Trouble. Hit us up if you need us," Yir said as they walked out the door. Throwing my hands over my face, I let out a loud yell.

"I fucked up, bro!" I said, turning to punch the wall. "I fucked up! I fucked up! I fucked up!" I shouted over and over fighting an invisible giant. I fucking lost her forever. A nigga been trying his best not to get hurt, but that shit ended up being the reason I got hurt. The way I treated her made her leave me for good. She was really about to marry that fucking nigga.

"Man, Ice kept telling you that shit. Nigga, just stay away from her. You just shot her with a fucking assault rifle. You could have fucking killed her. Just stay away from her cause I would hate to have to lay you down. We brothers, but I can't let one of us be out to get the other. You were dead wrong for that shit." I was about to fucking cry like a bitch, but when that nigga said that, everything left.

"Nigga you the last motherfucker to talk about right and wrong, Troub. I love her more than any other motherfucker walking this Earth, nigga. All jokes aside. I wasn't trying to fucking shoot her, but seeing her walking up there with that nigga I lost it, bro. I fucking snapped. I was on some psychotic shit. I would rather her be dead than with another nigga.

Seeing her fly back like that fucked me up, making me realize what the fuck I did. I would never fucking hurt Shanty like that, but she had me thinking crazy shit. I gotta get my mind right bro cause I can't function with her being with that nigga. I can't be near the shit," I said, and he nodded his head.

"So, what you thinking about doing?" he asked.

"I'm about to duck off to my junkyard and work to myself. Ion know who I can trust with my business no more, bro. I gotta be down for myself. I gotta get my shit together up top so that I can get over this shit and move on. A nigga gotta get Shanty out of my mind cause if I don't, I'm gone murder that nigga she's with," I said, making up my mind.

I'm laying low and focusing on my businesses. Ian even touching no work until I figure out who out for me. I already know the FEDs building a cause up against me. They got my presets already, so they're just trying to line up some niggas to turn on me so they can nail my ass. They'll never catch me slipping though. I'll leave all this shit alone before I go down.

"I'm out, I got to go get Lai from the hospital," Trouble said, walking out go my crib.

I turned and headed up the stairs to go lay the fuck down. This shit with Shanty got my fucking head hurting. Ion know what the fuck I'd do if I had killed Shanty. I gotta get her off my mind.

~

I stood off in the corner just watching her sleep. I know ian supposed to be off in here, but I just gotta get some shit off my chest. A nigga gotta let her go, but the shit is tough. Shanty is all I fucking know. She's been the one constant thing in a nigga's life. I could always count on her to ride for me at the end of the day. She was more than my fucking woman; she was my best friend, my rib, my fucking rider. She would lay a nigga down behind Fame, and the whole hood knows that shit. Now she down for another nigga and it's fucking me up. I can't take the shit. She started rolling in her sleep, and her eyes popped open immediately landing on me. I emerged from the shadows taking a seat in the chair beside her bed.

"Fame, I'm buzzing a fucking nurse!" she snapped, reaching for the button, but I reached over grabbing her hand.

"Chill Shanty and fucking listen. Them guards outside know I'm in here. Tell that nigga you with money can't buy everything. I know motherfuckers everywhere, and I get what I want— period. No one can keep you from me but me," I said, clenching my jaws. She had me getting pissed the fuck off, and that wasn't what the fuck I came in here for. Releasing her hand, I slid back in the chair taking a deep breath to calm my nerves.

"Do that nigga make you happy?" I asked, trying not to get mad at myself for fucking caring.

"Yea," she said with an attitude. I had to swallow my anger before replying.

"Ion always do shit right, but I love you. To me, that's all that fucking mattered. The fact that I love you was supposed to get us through shit. It was supposed to make up for all the shit I did," I said, and I knew she was rolling her eyes.

"That's why we weren't good together, Fame. You don't know how to love me," she said, and I agreed.

"I know I don't, but I'm gone learn. Even if it's too late, I'm still gone learn. I'm about to start working on me Shanty, and one day you'll wake up next to that nigga and realize he's just a placeholder. When you do, I'll be ready for us. Go be happy with that nigga. Make him show you what it's like to be loved right. That way when I get my shit together, you can tell me when I'm half stepping.

You can marry that nigga and do all that bullshit, but deep down you know you were made for me. He might be the better man, but I'm the right man for you, and that's what matters. I love you man, and I'm gone get my shit together. I'm gone fucking do that shit Shanty because I gotta be the man you end up with when our story ends," I let the bitch ass, tear slip, and I knew it was time to leave.

I kissed her lips before getting up and walking out of the room. I ignored the voice in my head telling me to kidnap her ass. I got in my car and let a few tears slip down my face. I'll never admit the shit but letting Shanty go hurts worse than my birth moms dying. This shit is rough but she deserves to be treated like a queen. That's something I wasn't doing. I wasn't honoring her as the only woman in my life, and that shit caused me to lose her. This shit is all on me, and I'm the only motherfucker that can fix it.

~

"AYYYYEEEEE YOOOO!" I heard Big Dee called out.

"I'm around to the left!" I shouted from underneath an old box Chevy.

I was working on a new compartment underneath. My last presets was to hit the brakes two times switch the wiper blades four times fast, and then turn on the radio. This time I've been working on something that unlocked by remote. I got a self-destruct function that will engage if you press the button three times fast. Then that shit locks up, and the only way to get back into it is to bring the shit to me.

"Nigga, you been ducked off! I had to go by your mom's crib to find out where you been hiding," he said as I rolled from under the car.

I wipe my hands on my jumper as I stood to my feet, to lean up against the car. Staring hard at him, I could tell that something was off about his ass. The nigga is acting suspect. Ion know if it's the fact that I know somebody's snaking me out, or if he's really on some fuck shit. Either way, something ain't all together with this nigga right now.

"What my OG say?"

"She told me yo ass was out here," he said looking everywhere but at me. Yea something is definitely off with this nigga. I'm gone play shit out like Ice is always talking about. I want to know for sure what's good with this nigga.

"I got some new presets. Come check these shits out," I said, and he followed me around the car.

"You heard from Vince? That nigga's been dodging my calls since you shut down shop. I've been trying to get at that nigga about some bread."

"Nah, ian been doing shit but chilling out here working and getting my mind right," he nodded, watching as I showed him the new presets.

I'm getting up with Vince later. I'm testing both of these niggas cause one of them is playing both sides. I finished showing Big Dee the shit before he headed out. After that, I started back fucking around on the cars thinking hard about this shit. I gotta figure out which one of my people are against me. My first mind is telling me to kill them both, but I owe them the benefit of the doubt. These two niggas have been down with me from the jump.

THREE

Markus Stringer

"You mean to tell me there was a shootout at the wedding, and you didn't use that opportunity to kill them all!" I shouted in anger. "All your targets were lined up together, and you passed on that chance!"

I can't fucking believe this shit. Incompetent is the only word that comes to mind for those imbeciles. How could they have everyone on the list in one place filled with gunfire and not take that opportunity? I've been trying to play the background, but it's time I took the forefront and handled this.

"Man, The Camp was there. Apparently, them niggas down with them now," Andre said with fear etched on his face. Our father is turning in his grave right now. Fear isn't something he instilled in us, especially not fear of man.

"Is that supposed to mean something to me?" I asked, standing to my feet. Brother or not I can't have a weakling in my ranks. That shit is a bad look.

"It does if you are planning to live long enough to see next week. Bro, I know you have your reasons for assigning us these tasks, but at the end of the day, these are your beefs. I will do what I was paid to do, and that's all. I'm not getting set up for a suicide mission. This shit you got planned out ain't gone end well for us, and I want out," Andre said, causing me to chuckle.

Years ago, my mother always told me that he would grow up to be a fucking disgrace and imagine my surprise that she was fucking right. Raising my gun, I put one right between his eyes.

"Does anyone else have any objections?" I asked the remaining three, and they each shook their heads no. "You are in charge. Do his job and yours with triple the results. Handle the other two situations and get me results! Forget bringing the bitch to me. I'll be seeing her personally." I pointed to the only one with the fucking guts to pull this shit off. I want that little bitch all for myself. She took everything that I cherished from me in one fucking day. I could never let her get off so easily.

"Wallace, Stinger! Today is your lucky day. You're on follow up calls," the captain said, dropping the folder onto my desk. Letting out an irritated sigh, I stood to my feet, grabbing my Glock, work cell, and the folder heading to the squad car.

"Just our fucking luck we get this shit when I have a fucking hangover," my partner complained.

"Captain's got it out of for us since that rich bitch called Judge Crocker on us," I said, pulling away from the station. "What's the first address?" He called off the address tot the hospital before reading me the case specifics. Hearing the details of the case, I knew that this shit was going to turn bad.

Captain was setting us up, and I knew it was because I fucked his daughter. He can't fault me for that. She showed up to the station waving her little ass in my face, so I filled her up with nine inches of hard pipe. Since then he's been up my ass about every little thing I do. I know he's waiting for the opportunity to send me up shit creek.

"Keep your lid on in here. This is a simple follow up, and that's all, Stinger. I would like to keep my shield for these last two months," Wallace said, and I nodded to placate him.

I do what I want, and he knows that. I'm sick of watching these rich entitles fucks game the system. We headed up to the room, and as soon as the mother let us in, I knew this shit was going to go left.

Just the look on the bitch's face as my partner spoke let me know that she felt her daughter did nothing wrong. I tried to keep my lid on, but I had to speak out.

I've had enough. These people have to start being held accountable for their bullshit.

"If I may be frank, we have gotten information that your daughter bullied the young lady at a party that happened the night of the accident, where your daughter manned the wheel of the car intoxicated, killing her friend. No offense, but I would hate to have a friend like her. Two deaths occur in a single high school, and your daughter is connected to both. I find it hard to believe she's as innocent as you claim. Well, I guess having money can clean the dirt off anything these days," I said with as much tact as my anger would allow.

From there the entire interview went left with the mother kicking us out, and the father threatening to have our shields. I knew that my ass was toast before hitting the elevator but right now, I don't give a shit. My phone rang, and I knew it was the captain. I picked up, and he was barking orders before I could speak.

"Get your asses to the station!" he shouted, hanging up.

"So much for my fucking pension," my partner mumbled, and I felt my gut rising.

I know the captain is nailing him to the cross right along with me, and that's never what I wanted. The drive to the station was a quiet one, and as soon as our asses touched the chair in the captain's office, he was shouting.

"I give you a task that a mall cop could complete and you still manage to fuck that up, Stinger. I'm getting calls from the fucking mayor about one of my detective mouthing off to one of his biggest contributors. You pull that shit in the projects with those street rats, but not in the biggest hospital in the fucking city. That's it, you're both done! Turn over your badge and weapons and pray that I don't figure out a way to make sure the only job you get is flipping fucking burgers!" he spat, and I laughed to myself.

"Something funny, Stinger?" he challenged.

"I was just laughing at how you just freed up all my time to go and fuck you daughter. Hell, I may even give your wife a round or two. We all know that tight pussy of hers is need of some actions with you too busy fucking the street rats as you call them," I said, wishing he'd run up. I had been waiting to put my glock against his head; since day he ruined my career the first time.

"Get your ass out of my office before I end your pathetic life," he threatened.

I tossed my badge on his desk. Quickly pulling my weapon. I aimed it at him and he looked like he was about to shit a brick. I laughed, tossing it on his desk. Fuck this job. I walked out of the station not even bothering to grab anything off my desk; they could trash all of that shit. That night I went home and took out my frustration deep inside of my wife's womb.

After that, my partner sunk into a deep depression, burying himself inside the bottle. Six months later, he died of liver sclerosis. That was a hard pill for me to swallow especially since my wife had been on my back heavily about me not finding work. She didn't know that I was running my father's empire, but soon after the money enlightened her. I waited years to my hands on that Malaika. At first, no one would turn on her, but pretty soon all the ducks lined up pretty nicely. So many people hate the little bitch that I don't think she'll see any of it coming.

FOUR

Niyah

Struggling to gain consciousness, I opened my eyes clutching my head. Touching the back of it, I felt a wet yet thick substance, and the area was tender. I frantically looked at my hands noticing they were covered in my blood. *What in the fuck happened to me?* One minute, I'm calling an ambulance, and the next I'm waking up with a bleeding head. Looking around, I realized I was in an unfamiliar place. Where ever I am is nice as fuck. This bed feels like heaven, and the sheet must be Egyptian cotton.

"You like that shit, huh?" a familiar voice said.

I looked around in search of him. Looking to the left, I noticed Ice leaned up against the wall in an all-black Armani suit. He looked so damn sexy that I forgot all about my aching head. I found myself hiking up my dress gesturing for him to come get some. He rushed over snatching me up by the hair causing a sharp and unbearable pain to shoot through my head.

"Bitch, you must have lost your fucking mind," he gritted, yanking me from the bed and tossing me on the floor.

My head started pounding like a fucking drum. I just laid there wondering what this was all about. The only thing that came to mind was that he must know I was sent to set him up. It's really nothing personal. I love Ice, but some things are more important than love.

"Get the fuck up. I'm taking you on a tour," he said literally snatching me out of my thoughts. He pushed me out of the room and into the hallway. "This was supposed to be our new home. I hope you like the shit since you'll be buried out back," he said, sending chills up my spine. This wasn't the Ice I know. This nigga was on some crazy shit right now.

"Ice, just let me explain," I said, causing him to laugh.

"That's the same shit the last bitch said. That shit didn't work, but check out the crown molding though," he said, pointing upwards. I can't lie like I wasn't nice, but my fear made it hard to focus.

He guided me through the halls showing me each room. There were nine bedrooms in total, with a mini nail salon set up for me, and his own personal gym. We both had offices and a lounge room; he referred to his as a man cave. The house is gorgeous. Knowing that he did all this for me touches my heart. I wish circumstances were different because I know that Ice is the man that I'm meant to be with.

"You know when Ali played me, I sat up there trying to find the words for why I was hurt, but to be real, I wasn't all that hurt. I felt played, but that shit didn't cut me deep," he said as we headed down to the basement.

He led me to an empty room with concrete floors and a drain in the center. It looks like it's supposed to be a bathroom or something like that. "You though, Ni. This shit with you cutting a nigga deep. I thought we were better than this shit. You could have come to me about any fucking thing."

"Everything ain't that damn easy!" I spat.

"It could have been if you fucking trusted in me! IN ME! Why the fuck would you turn against me, Ni? Or were you against me from the jump? What that nigga sent Ali because you couldn't do the job?" he gritted, stepping towards me like he was about to lay my ass out.

"No! I didn't even know that bitch. Say what you want Ice, but you know I fucking love you. You're telling me to trust in you, but how about you trust in me! Shit looks bad, but I have my reasons. I would never just set you up, even before we got back together, but I had no choice," I cried reaching out to him, and he pulled his gun on me.

"And ion have a choice neither," he gritted, cocking the hammer.

"He'll kill my son if I don't help him get to you!" I blurted with my eyes closed tightly waiting for the bullet to end my life, but it never came. I peeped through one eye, and he was just staring at me with tears in his eyes.

"I want to fucking kill you so bad, Ni. I want to put one straight through your fucking skull, but something is telling me to get answers. You got one chance to tell me what the fuck is up or it's a wrap for you," he said, and I knew I had to come clean.

"Can you at least get me some pain pills and let me lay down, first?"

"Bitch, does it look like I'm taking requests? Get to talking!" he demanded.

"Ok! I went to Andre because I needed his help," I talked slowly try to stall, but he caught on immediately. He sent a bullet flying past my head, compelling me to cut the bullshit. "I got in with Andre because he has sway with the judges in family court, and I needed them in order to gain custody of my son. At first, he had me finessing niggas for him. He'd pay me a portion, keeping the majority for himself. He said if I did it for long enough, I'd gain his trust and he'd help me get my son."

"The fuck any of this has to do with me?" he snapped like he didn't believe a word I had to say.

"I don't know. He approached me months ago about you. He told me he had a long job for me, and I politely declined, especially after that nigga showed me your picture. I had plans on coming to tell you about the shit as soon as he dropped me off until I saw the other picture he had in the folder. Some kind of way he got to my son. He took a picture with my baby and showed it to me as proof that he could get to him if I didn't go along with the plan," I said, feeling tears fall down my face. Lowering the gun, he put it on safety before tucking it behind his back as he walked out the room locking me in.

I sat with my back against the wall thinking. So much has changed since I've been back with Ice. It's like he's been the positive force I needed to strive for better. My parents taking my son from me made me cold on the inside. I stopped giving a fuck about anybody and made it my mission to stack up money to get him back, but no matter how much money I stacked, I could never trump the clout my parents have. That's why I needed Andre. He was connected to so many affluent men because of his little escort service. I knew working for him would pay off in the end. All I want is my baby back, I want him back more than I want air in my lungs.

I got pregnant on my very first time having sex. I was a sophomore at the time, and I hid my entire pregnancy. I thank God nothing went wrong because I gave birth to him at the bathroom of Lai's house. I still remember the looks on her and Sheila's faces as I pushed him out. They were so damn scared, but they never left me. They helped me bring Anju into the world safe and sound.

The moment I laid eyes on him, I knew I'd love him forever. I also knew that having him meant my family had to accept him. I just knew that I was going to keep my baby. I had my parent fucked all the way up because they showed up to the hospital on good bullshit. My mother came into the room, rattling off instructions to the doctors while my father sat back staring at me with disgust.

He had hopes of me becoming a so much more, but everyone makes mistakes, right? They always put so much pressure on me to revolutionize the family business. My father had so much faith in me, but I never wanted any of that. I mean what child wants to become a cryptographer. Shit, what child knows what the fuck that shit is. I always had to make the best grades, especially in math and science. My father pushed and pushed and pushed, until one day I started to hang with the cool girls. Hanging out turned into doing the shit they did and my ass got knocked up. The boy I got pregnant by abandoned me because he was scared of his parents too. Having my son gave me the confidence I needed to stop cowering to my parents overbearing ways. I guess they knew that too because they ripped him right from my arms.

The day I gave birth, my parents had them come to take my baby away to be raised by someone they hired. They wanted to bury any proof of me ever giving birth. Some kind of way, they took custody of my son and made him disappear. If I were lucky, they'd show me pictures, promising to give him back if I followed their rules. That shit worked for a long ass time until I graduated high school and realized they weren't giving Anju back. I had to get on my independent shit and go fight for my fucking son. Shit, I even thought about torturing their asses for the information on him.

The sickest part of it all is my ass father still sends me pictures of Anju to taunt me. I don't know how Andre found out where they have him, but seeing him with those pictures, I knew I had to do whatever he said to get closer to getting my son. I was desperate, and at this point, I have to get him whether it be legal or illegal, I need him with me. I just pray Ice doesn't come back and kill my ass before I can get to see him again.

FIVE

Trouble

"Fuck this dick, bitch!" I grunted as Lai threw her ass back on my shit.

Watching her plump, little ass bounce on me had my dick long as the Nile River. Grabbing her hips, I slammed her deeper on my dick, admiring how she still kept her deep arch. Lai was a pro at taking the dick, and she had a nigga ready to drink her dirty bath water.

"Fuck! Give it to me daddy," she moaned, sounding like a white bitch.

"Nah! Dirty that shit up," I commanded, smacking her ass cheeks with one hand and yanking her hair with the other. I fucked her harder, and she started screaming out begging for mercy, but Trouble don't spare no souls.

"What the fuck I say!"

SMACK! SMACK! POP!

"SHITTTTTTT! Fuck me harder you stupid bitch!" she shouted.

"That's what the fuck I'm talking about," I gritted, flipping her over.

I grabbed both her ankles in one hand, and I pinned them up against the headboard. That pretty pussy was staring right at me, and I could help but kiss it. I licked and sucked her pussy so good I had her hitting opera notes.

"Please! I can't take it no more," she begged for the tenth time.

She tasted so good that I can't get enough of her. Lai got a nigga eating ass and all that shit. Taking my tongue, I stuck it deep in her pussy, slurping all the juices only to be washed up in her tidal waves. My bitch is wetter than the ocean! Shit! Giving her what she wants I buried myself deep in her womb. She was coming back to back, but I was still going strong, beasting in that pussy. She had me feeling like Hercules, and her pussy was my source of strength.

"Tell me what the dick is, Lai?" I commanded. It took her too long to find her voice, so I pulled out shoving myself into her hard and fast. I did it five more times with her screaming out and shaking.

"OOHHHHHH! This dick is TROUBBLLEEEEEE!" she screamed out as she splattered cum all over my stomach. That shit had me coming so hard that I thought I burst a blood vessel in my eye. I fell over ready to go to sleep, but Lai's talkative ass was ready to start up.

"Donavan," she said softly. I know this about to be some emotional shit cause she calling me Donavan.

"Malaika don't start asking me fifty fucking question. Go to sleep!" I demanded, praying that the roughness of my tone would shut her the fuck up.

"I was just asking one damn question!" she snapped back, causing me to shoot my head in her direction.

"Watch your fucking mouth."

"Watch yours," she retorted, and I grabbed her up by the back of her neck pulling her so that we were nose to nose.

"What the fuck you want, before I slap you for your smart ass mouth," I said, looking her in the eyes. She rolled her eyes, smacking her lips, and doing every fucking thing but asking the question. Ion know what the fuck has gotten into her, but this ain't my bitch right here. She's been hanging with Shanty and Niyah too fucking much planning that damn wedding. They got her catching attitudes and talking out of line.

"Say what you gotta say," I ordered, tightening my grip on her hair.

"I was just going to say that. I was going to my friend's memorial tomorrow."

"You not going nowhere. Somebody is still out for you, and until I find that nigga, we're laying low. This shit at the wedding was enough stress for me right now."

"I wasn't asking! Last time I check I was free now, meaning I can go where ever I want." I swear I had twelve niggas in my head whispering for me to choke the life out of this bitch. This smart mouth shit ain't gone fly.

"I said NO! Shut the fuck up about it and take your ass to sleep, Malaika."

When I tell her something she's gotta roll with the shit I say because I know what's fucking best. The fuck I look like allowing her to go to some shit that whoever after her knows she will be at. That's like walking her into the lion's den in a meat vest. Any halfway decent shooter can put one in her dome the minute she exits the car. That shit is an automatic hell no. She rolled over huffing and puffing, and then the fucking tears started up. I got up and head up to my office. Lai ain't about to play that shit with me. She's not going to that shit and its fucking final.

"Stay in the fucking car while I got scope shit out," I said mad that I even brought her ass up here.

She played a nigga good. As soon as I laid down, she hit me with more tears, making me put her ass out of bed. Then she started cutting the fuck up. I figured if I didn't bring her ass here I would end up snapping her fucking neck. She got five minutes to send the Hail Mary's up to that dead bitch, and we out of here. It's too many vantage points out here to just have out here longer. The high winds are the only thing in our fucking favor right now.

I scope the area, and everything seems legit. It wasn't but six people at this shit and I personal patted each on down. Ian give a fuck about the attitudes they were shooting neither. The bitch has been died for over five years, so they ain't all that fucking hurt. Plus, they might be after Lai for all I know she did kill the bitch, so it ain't that farfetched to believe that shit. *I'm gone check into that when I get back home.*

"Hurry up and get this shit over with," I said, opening her car door. She got out of the car, and I stood back at the road keeping an eye on shit from a distance.

I was watching the way her ass was bouncing as she walked to the grave. I damn near bent her over one of these tombstones. She needs to hurry up. I'm fucking horny as fuck. Lai got about five paces in before shit went left. The old bitch tried to swing on her while two niggas barely held her back. I rushed over there ready to lay everybody down if that old bitch touches her.

"Why would you come here? You are not welcomed here?" the old bitch screamed out.

Some nigga wrapped his arms around Lai carrying her off, and I turned into the roadrunner getting to them. I instantly snatched her out of his arms, moving her aside while I put that nigga on his head.

"Fuck wrong with you touching her, nigga?" I gritted with my gun aimed at his temple. The nigga started scrambling to answer like I really gave a fuck. I pulled the trigger, but Lai pushed my arm causing the bullet to hit the dirt.

"What are you doing? That's my friend. He was trying to protect me from her!" she screamed.

"You lucky, nigga," I said with a light chuckle before dragging her ass away.

"The fuck you mean protecting you! It ain't no nigga job to protect you but mine, don't fucking let no nigga touch on you period," I ranted, pulling her to the car by her arm.

I made sure to get a look at every muh'fucka out there. All of them got some shit coming their way for trying to ambush her. They weren't holding that old bitch back they were faking the funk. Them niggas wanted her to lay hands on Lai, and for that I'm laying hands on they asses.

I didn't have shit to say the whole time I was driving back to the crib. She was sitting her dumb ass in the passenger seat crying over shit she brought on herself. She came to some shit that she knew she wasn't welcomed at. The fuck she thought was gone happen. What they was gone magically forget that she killed the dead bitch. Lai be acting stupid.

"Cut all that crying out. You did this shit to yourself. The fuck you go somewhere you know they ain't want you to be at for?"

"Because I have to pay my respects too; I have to apologize to them every chance I get. I need their forgiveness!" she shouted, and I just shook my head at how dumb she sounded.

"You don't need shit from them fucking people. Accept the fact that you fucked up and they might not ever forgive yo ass. You're going to depression sessions and shit when you ain't fucking depressed. Yo ass in fucking denial!" I barked, and she looked upside my head.

"You don't know what I'm feeling. Just shut the fuck up!" Before I knew it, my hands were locked around her neck.

"I'm close to chaining you back up! You acted with more common sense then," I said, looking from her to the road. She got me putting hands on her in the middle of the fucking expressway. Muh'fuckas in Dallas can't drive good enough for her to be pissing me off like this.

"Let me go! You're hurting me," she cried, dropping the attitude. I pushed her head away from me and continued to drive.

I'm dropping her ass off at her house, and she better not fucking leave until I get back. Pulling up outside of her apartment complex, I waited on her to get the fuck out, but again she was trying me. Lai knows ian use to all this attitude shit she's got going on. I'll fuck around and slap her ass unconscious. She needs to just get the fuck out before I lay hands on her. I'm trying to get some air and cool off, but she's pushing a nigga.

"Lai, get the fuck out!"

"No! We have to talk about this," she said.

"Ain't shit to talk about. I say you fucking do, period. Get the fuck out the car before I slang your ass out on the pavement. Ian got time for this shit; I got shit I need to do."

"You can do it after we discuss our issues."

"What issues?" I barked, bringing my face nose to nose with hers. She had me so fucking mad that I had smoke coming from my ears.

"The fact that you think you own me and that you talk to me any type of way," she said so low that I barely heard her ass.

"Get the fuck out of my truck. This is my last time saying the shit before I lay hands on you." She let tears slip as she turned rushing to open her door. It took her a five damn minute to grab her purse and get out. She was doing too fucking much.

"You know what, I never asked for any of this, and right now I can do without it," she said before slamming the door.

I had to take a deep breath because I was about to get out and knock her ass out. She's stressing me the fuck out. I gotta go get some pussy before I handle this bullshit. I turned my car on heading down to get some pussy from the old bitch with the gambling ring. I'm supposed to be picking a Black Panther from a private hangar on the outskirts of the city, but my head so fucked up right now I'd kill somebody just to release some anger.

"I knew you'd be back," the old bitch said when I stepped through her door.

My response was to snatch her up b her hand and shove her against the wall filling her up with dick. I roughly fucked that bitch for a few hours until she passed out. We went through a box of condoms, and I was still in a fucked up mood. I might just stay the fuck away from Lai for a while. Maybe then, she'll learn how to shut the fuck up sometimes.

SIX

Ice

This bitch is out of her fucking mind if she thinks I believe anything that comes out of her fucking mouth. She told a good story, but I barely believe the bitch. If it wasn't about a child being involved, I would have killed her off principle. I fucking love that bitch, and she did the same shit as Ali. That shit ain't sitting right in me. It got me feeling all fucked up. She had me on some Trouble type of shit. I've never wanted to lay hands on a woman more than I wanted to punch her in the fucking mouth. I got out of the car and headed up to Lai's apartment. Troub said she's here, and I need to verify this shit Niyah was talking. Knocking on the door hard as hell, I waited for her to open it.

"What?" she shouted, snatching the door open, but the sight of me calmed her down. I guess she was expecting somebody else. Nine times out of ten Trouble fucked up.

"Hey sis, can I holler at you about something?" She moved aside allowing me in. I took a seat on one of her couches and she sat on the one across from me.

"Niyah says she got a son, and I'm trying to see how true that is," I got straight to the point, not wanting to prolong this shit. She looked at me like she was battling with telling me or not.

"The truth is what could save her fucking life," I said aggressively. I know Ni is her homegirl and she trying not to drop the dime on her, but lying gone get her ass a bullet. Then who knows what will happen to the kid if he exists.

"Yes, she has a son. His name is Anju. I actually help her with hiding the pregnancy. I felt bad because I hooked her up with the guy. I was a bitch back in high school. I wasn't a virgin, so I pressured my friends to lose their virginity too. She didn't want to be outcasted, so she did to be in with me," she said, and I just sat there looking at her. I wanted her to get to the fucking point, but sis sounds like she gotta get this shit off her chest.

"When she had him, we thought that her parents would be accepting of him. You know once he was already in the world, but they weren't. They took her baby and used him to keep her on track with their goals for her. All of our parents had so many high hopes for us.

Niyah's parents own a company that creates algorithms for defense weapons. You know like the GPS trackers in missiles that help them hit their targets and stuff like that. They wanted that for her, but she had other dreams. So in a sense, I guess having Anju was a blessing in disguise to them because they knew it would be a tool to keep her where they wanted her," she said.

"So how the fuck she end up stripping?"

"She started realizing that they were never going to give her son back. I mean how would that look. Niyah's parents are just like mine; everything is about their appearance and reputation. They couldn't have everyone knowing that their child was a teen mother. She knew that no matter what they'd always keep Anju away, so she started trying to get him back legally. That was a disaster. The court system is corrupt, and judges can be bought, and that what they did. She wasn't a stripper at first. She was in college doing what they wanted.

She had a nice apartment and more than enough money to care for her son, but that meant nothing. So, she gave it all up and started searching for ways to game the system just like they did. Niyah wasn't always loud and bitchy. She was the sweetest thing, but having your own parents rip your child from your arms then use him to manipulate you, changes a person. She became all about herself, and I can't say I blame her. She wasn't lying about Anju, but you know that because you wouldn't have come to ask if you didn't even slightly believe her," she said, calling me on my shit. I chuckled.

"Yea, I guess you right sis, but ian fucking with her like that right now," I said, and she sighed.

"Whatever she did don't hold it heavily against her. Niyah has a system that she lives by, she tries to keep people away, but she cares. I know that she has her ways, but she loves you. Just don't hold things against her," I nodded, but I wasn't hearing that shit. She couldn't love a nigga too much cause she played the fuck out of me.

There's always another way. It might be risky, but that where trust comes in at. All Ni had to do was trust me from the jump, and I could've got her son back. Ion know how, but I would have done that shit just like I'm going to do now.

"Yea, sis. I hear you, but I gotta go get up with some people. Stay safe sis, Trouble said lock up." Mentioning Trouble made her roll her eyes, causing me to laugh. As I was walking out, some nigga was walking up to her door. That shit had me looking at her in a way now.

"Say homie, who the fuck is you?" I barked walking up on him.

"I'm Jacob, an old friend of Malaika. I'm just here to check on her after what happened earlier," he said.

"It's ok Ice. I know him," she quickly interrupted.

"I see that, but what I'm trying to get at is how well. Shit, let me get up with bro to see," I said, pulling out my phone.

They're crazy as fuck to think I'm leaving him outside her door. They say birds of a feather and Ni a fraud so Lai might be too. Shit, Shanty was getting dick on the side, and I would have never guessed that shit.

"Aye bro, I'm outside Lai's crib and some nigga outchea talking about they friends."

"I'm pulling up now." The tone of his voice let me know it was about to be some shit. I walked off meeting my bro in the parking lot. We slapped hands, and I continued to my car while he headed up. That's their shit and ian trying to be involved in it. I got other shit to handle.

"I think that nigga's taking a dirt nap. We watched homie pull into a mansion, but he ain't never pull out. You know what that shit means," Archie said with Gip nodding.

"Arch was on him that day, so all I can do is go with his word, but I will say that he ain't been around his little side business in a few days. Whatever his part was in the shit, it wasn't that deep cause homie gone," Gip added.

"We need to be looking into who owns that crib he was at. It seems like that's who he was answering to," Archie said. I just sat back listening.

"Archie, you get on that. Matter of fact, camp outside of that bitch until you can come up with answers." He nodded, walking out of the room.

I looked at Gip taking a deep breath. "I got some shit that needs to be handled, but it gotta stay between us. It's a kid involved, and I can't risk him getting hurt in the fallout."

"Say no more," he said. I filled him in on shit, and he left to get right to it. Gip used to be in the army, but the nigga got booted out for fighting his commanding officer. Ever since then he's been my right hand. If Gip can't get shit done, it can't be done, period.

I turned on the radio heading back to the house to let Ni's ass out of the basement. She pissed me off so bad that I snapped and pulled some shit Troub would do. I would never lock a woman in a damn room. Shit, I almost forget she was still down there. As soon as I opened the fucking door to the room, the smell of piss hit me hard as fuck.

"Yo, what the fuck Ni?" I barked. She hopped up raining blows on a nigga.

"You crazy motherfucker!" she shouted, fighting the fuck out of me. I fell back to the wall, trying to pull her wild ass back without knocking the fuck out of her. She clocked my ass one time in the eye, and that was it. I backhanded her sending her tumbling to the floor, screaming and crying.

"I fucking hate your stupid ass!" she screamed like she wasn't setting me up to get fucking killed. Regardless of the fact ian sorry for my actions because how else was I supposed to fucking treat her.

"Get off the fucking floor and go get cleaned up. You got shit to do!" I barked, and she looked up at me with tears staining her face. Her cheek was fire red and her eyes matched. I felt a pang of guilt for hitting her. It quickly went away as soon as she opened her loud ass mouth.

"Ian got shit to do! You locked me the fuck up down here for all that fucking time! I'm hungry and fucking thirsty!" she snapped.

"Just do what the fuck I said, Niyah!" I shouted, causing her to jump.

Being down here got her ass thinking that I won't fucking kill her. I won't, but she needs to tread fucking lightly. In her fucking mind, she needs to be scared that I'll snap her neck at any moment. She ran up the stairs, and I followed. I already had Greta cooking lunch, but she's not eating until she washes her ass. The stench of piss is all over her.

"Did you piss on yourself?"

"No, I pissed down that fucking drain. The fuck I look like pissing on myself? I was scared, but not that gah damn scared!" she snapped, looking at me crazy. I pushed her towards the stairs leading to the since floor.

"Go wash yo ass and hurry up." She rushed up the stairs while I headed to my office to check into some shit.

I got a plan for these niggas who want to cross me. I'm going to give them niggas just what they're asking for, and I'll use Niyah's fraud ass to do it. The only way for her to prove her loyalty to me is for her to bring me the niggas out to get me. If she can't do that, her son gone be a fucking orphan. Like I said before, I made the mistake of trusting a snake ass bitch once, but it'll never happen twice.

SEVEN

Lai

"What are you doing here?" I asked, pulling Jacob inside of my apartment. Making sure to lock the door, I know Trouble is probably on his way, and I really want to talk to Jacob.

"I came to check on you that's all. After what happened at the memorial, I was worried. That guy snatched you out of there pretty quick," he said, and I shook back the tears. Trouble put me in such a bad mood that I barely had any time to process what had happened.

"I just want your family to know how deeply sorry I am. Jacob, I know I was a horrible person then, but I'm not that way anymore."

"I know, and I'm pretty sure they do too, but they just need someone to blame. If it makes you feel any better, I think I've successfully got booted from the family. They found my coke, and now I'm homeless," he said, shoving his hands into his pockets and looking off towards the ground.

"You can stay here with me," I offered, and he looked up with a huge smile, grabbing me in for a hug. Before we could finish our conversation, Trouble kicked my front door in. The sight of me in

Jacob's arm sent him further over the edge, and he snatched us apart, sending me flying over the couch. I could hear him attacking Jacob. Quickly, I jumped up screaming for him to stop so I could explain.

"DONAVAN, STOP!" I shouted, but he wasn't hearing me.

Fearing that he might kill him, I grabbed my cheap lamp and broke it over his head. I didn't nothing to disorient him, but it did catch his attention. He stilled slightly, reaching around to touch his bloodied wound. In an instant, he was on me, choking the life from my body. I frantically clawed at his arms, doing everything to get him off me, but his frame was massive on top of mine.

"You're killing her! We were just talking I hugged her because she offered me a place to stay. My parents kicked me out," Jacob slurred in the distance.

No longer having the strength I stopped fighting, staring him deep into his eyes in a final plea. His hollow eyes stared back and just as I felt myself slip, life flashed through his eyes. As if he finally realized that it was me he was hurting, he released me standing to his feet.

"Get the fuck out!" he barked, speaking to Jacob. I didn't have the strength to look, but I could hear Jacob scrambling to his feet and bolting out of the apartment. I struggled to sit up, but I was too lightheaded.

"Bitch, you lost your fucking mind?" he asked, stepping in front of me. All I could do was look up at him. His large frame towered mine and his stance was very aggressive. I could feel his anger as he stood holding a towel to his head.

"You were going to kill him," I whispered. A pang of fear hit me as I was speaking. I'm a singer so quite naturally I was worried about my voice.

"You should have thought about that shit before you had him in here!" he barked, causing me to jump. "I swear you want me to lock you up. This shit's got me fucked up in the head!" he shouted, stepping closer to me as I sat up against the back of the couch. It was then that I got a whiff of a cheap fragrance. It's like the scent filled the air at that point. It was cotton candy, a scent I wouldn't dare wear. Finally getting a good amount of air back into my system I stood to my feet.

"Where did you just come from?" My question shocked him, and he stared at me as if he was thinking about something.

"Get out of my face and go get some shit so we can go!"

I knew better than to disobey, so I headed into the room, grabbing my notebook and guitar. The more I moved the more my feelings start to get the better of me. He cheated on me. I don't even know what to believe at this point. I've fooled myself into thinking that this man loves me, but he can't possibly if it was just so easy for him to go fuck another woman. He thinks he has me in line, but I'm going to show him better than I can tell him. I will not be trapped in this crazy ass relationship. Out of all the other shit, he does to me, cheating won't be added to the list. Grabbing the rest of my things, I sucked back my tears and heading out the door, feeling more determined with each step.

"Bitch, what you should have done was beat his ass with that heavy ass guitar you got!" Niyah snapped through the phone. Trouble left his phone with me, so I used it to call them.

"Niyah, what should you have done when Ice locked you up and had you pissing down that drain?" Shanty snapped back in my defense.

"See bitch them is new wounds!" Niyah snapped back.

I rolled my eyes cause this simple conversation will take all day. All I wanted is to vent, and they're arguing over stupid shit. Keeping them on subject is a full-time job. I just sat back listening to the throw insults back and forth until I had enough.

"OKAY! I called the two of you to talk about my damn feelings, and you bitches are only concerned about yourselves! I swear you have me wanting to go back to my old ways," I fussed, and they laughed.

"You see how you just spoke yo fucking mind to us. That's the same shit you need to do with Trouble," Niyah said, and I wanted to reach through the phone and choke her ass like Bill Cosby in *Ghost Dad*. Her mouth just never stops sometimes.

"Niyah shut the fuck up, bitch. You need to go suck Ice's dick to cool your ass off. Ian got but a good twenty more minutes before Neron comes in here and realizes I sent the physical therapist packing. So, spill all the tea, Lai," Shanty said, and I immediately went into telling them about what transpired the day of Sheila's memorial. From how he choked me and beat the shit out of Jacob, to smelling that cheap perfume on him. When I was finished, I felt relieved and hurt at the same time. It was like I had just smelled the scent all over again. I don't think I've ever been this hurt by a man's actions. Donavan takes me through too many waves.

"Lai, you gotta stop being so damn scared of Trouble," Shanty said in a serious tone.

"Bitch! Be afraid! Be veryyyyyyy afraid! Ion know what the fuck is wrong with Shantalya acting like that nigga ain't certifiable but please don't listen to this girl." Niyah snapped cutting Shanty off.

"Bitch I'm about to hop on a flight and come fuck yo ass up! I was getting to my fucking point gah damn. Like I was saying, LAI!" Shanty shouted, emphasizing my name. "Stop being so afraid of him. Trouble's not gone hurt you for real. He might fuck you up, but he won't kill you. So, stop being timid around him and nut the fuck up. Yo ass been living in the hood long enough you know how to get with the shits."

"You know what I knew this bitch was good for something. I'm gone give you your props Shanty cause you're right for once. I agree with that Lai. Since Ice got me on lockdown doing hard time, I've been up on my Kindle reading and shit. You gotta get like that bitch British from A.J. Davidson's book *Cherished by a Boss*. She's fucking with this crazy nigga and that bitch gets just as crazy. Every time Trouble chokes yo ass get on top of him in his sleep and choke his ass. Ion care what Shanty say don't fuck with that nigga while he up and aware," Niyah joked.

"I don't know how to be like that," I said slowly feeling sadness come over me. "I love him, and he just cheated on me so easily," I responded feeling lower than low.

"First off, I don't think Trouble knows what it is to be in a relationship. The only woman Trouble was anywhere close to being with is Debbie. She's got a gambling ring in Oak Cliff, and she lets it be known that her and Trouble been messing around for years. Back to the point though, you are the first woman that Trouble really loves. You gotta teach him certain shit, one being that he can't just treat you any type of way.

I made the mistake of letting Fame get away with shit, and look how we ended up. Don't let Trouble fuck up your mental like Fame did mine. When he fucks up, you nut up and that's real. Stop being weak and boss the fuck up. Go by Mama Rosemary's house, get my Kindle from my old room, and read all of the books by Mz. Lady P and Mz. Lady P Presents. You gone know exactly how to handle that nigga." Before I could respond, Trouble walked into the room.

"Yea Shanty, I think we should all go out when you come back."

"Bitch, you should have hung up. Make his ass think a nigga was on the phone," Niyah said, causing her and Shanty to laugh.

"Ok, I'll talk to y'all later."

"If something pops off, do a bird call, and Niyah will bust down yo door." Shanty said and I held in my laugh, hanging up on them. Sometimes I wonder why I even call them for advice because they are both stupid.

"You ain't cook, shit?" he asked as he undressed.

My mouth watered as soon as he pulled his hoodie and shirt off. He was so sexy that it took my mind to better places. Places where he didn't hurt me in the first few months of us being together. In this place, we met on better terms, and he never kidnapped nor abused me, but like all good things, the fantasy faded when he opened his mouth.

"Do you hear me talking?"

"No, I thought that you would be eating cotton candy," I said with a slight smirk.

"The fuck is you talking about?" he snapped, and I turned my head to hide my laugh.

"Nothing, I didn't cook anything. I was actually about to head to your mom's house." He stopped emptying his pockets to stare at me questionably. I responded with a blank stare and slight smile. Being sneaky is the one thing I have mastered.

"Bring back a plate of whatever she cooked since you ain't do shit all day!" he snapped. "Straight there and back. Shit is quiet for now, but that doesn't mean niggas ain't plotting," he said, walking into the bathroom to shower.

Rushing out the door, I headed straight to the Apple store to get the new iPhone. I had them set it all up for me before heading to Mama Rosemary's.

"Chile, where the hell you done been. That damn Trouble's been calling me for two hours looking for you. Hell, looks like he done found you," she said, pointing behind me.

Trouble was pulling up the street. A part of me was afraid, but I was mostly ok with the choice I made. I had to go out and get a phone so that I could create a Facebook page to get in touch with Jacob. I've been feeling like shit not knowing if he was ok. With his parents cutting him off, there's only a matter of time before he ends up on the streets, especially since his parents blew through his and Sheila's trust funds when we were in high school. They're living off the money from her life insurance policy right now. Jacob is ass out, and I feel a sense of responsibility for him.

"Where did you go?" she asked in a rush as he was pulling into her driveway.

"To the mall. I went to get a phone, but I don't want him to know," I said, and she nodded.

"Follow my lead."

Getting out of the car shirtless in basketball shorts and Nike slides, he made his way to us. I could tell he was upset from his stance. His shoulders were tense, and his brows were furrowed. He was so sexy, but I always think that.

"What the hell you rushing up here huffing and puffing fa! I told you she was out running errands for me. What you don't trust my word now?"

"What errand you got that had her in the mall?"

"Head on inside and let me talk to my son," she said, and I happily rushed through the doors.

I headed up to Shanty's bedroom grabbing her Kindle. I snuggled on a sofa in the living room and started reading the *Love & War* series by Latoya Nicole. I got so caught up in the book that I didn't even notice him come in until he was telling me to get my stuff. I followed him to the house and went straight to the couch to finish the book. I was taking notes and learning. Pretty soon I'll know exactly what the fuck bossing up even means. I didn't want to sound lame by telling Shanty and Niyah I didn't know. They'd never let me live that down.

EIGHT

Shanty

"Let me sit this ass on you, show you how I feel
Let me take this off, will you watch me
Yes, mass appeal
Don't take your eyes, don't take your eyes off it
Watch it, babe
If you like, you can touch me baby."

Seductively I sashayed over to the chair I placed in the center of the floor as Beyoncé's "Rocket" played through the speakers. I had on a black sheer lace bodysuit that has a thong panty. On my feet were hot pink patent leather red bottoms. My hair was in spiral curls with a deep side bang. I did a pink lip because Neron thinks pink is super sexy on me. I eased over towards him swirling my hip. I spent hours while he was on calls learning the routine.

As I moved to the beat, I could see the lust in his eyes for me; small licks of the lips and fist clenches gave away his arousal. Just knowing that I was turning him on fueled me to go harder. You would never think my arm is in a sling with the way I'm working the floor for my man. Turning around, I bent over giving him a full shot of my fat ass. I heard him suck air into his mouth and the next thing I knew he was lifting me off my feet.

I had a whole routine planned out, finishing with a lap dance, but ian mad if he wants to skip to the good shit. I wrapped my legs around him as he ripped my body suit at the crouch. His aggressiveness is shocking, but again a bitch aint mad at all. *Take this pussy daddy and fuck me hard!* Taking me over to the bed, he laid me down and freed all that big meat.

Neron's dick is so fucking chocolate and gorgeous that I want to go to sleep and wake up with it in my mouth. My pussy was running like a scary bitch caught fucking her best friend's man. I was so fucking wet for this nigga. He entered me, taking my breath away. Leaving no time for me to adjust, he began to fuck me down, up, and around. He had my pussy doing the Harlem shake!

"That's my spot!" I moaned, and he leaned upright, grabbing me by my neck choking me softly but firmly.

"Cum for me!" he demanded, but I was stuck in the orgasmic high. My pussy was tingling as he fucked me harder.

"NOW!" he roared, shattering the last of my restraint. I came so hard that I started swinging and fighting. He's trying to kill me by fucking me this damn good.

"We're not done yet," he said, flipping me over and smacking me hard on the ass. That shit had my pussy thumping. For hours, he fucked me down and if we weren't in the penthouse suite, I know we'd be getting noise complaints.

As usual, we laid in bed after some amazing ass sex tangled up in each other. Neron's long limbs were wrapped around me interlaced in mine as he held me close slowly rubbing the burn on my thigh. It's something that I've grown oddly accustomed to. Like a bitch wakes up out my sleep to make him start back when he stops. He spoils me in every single damn way.

"What are we doing tomorrow? I want to actually see Italy before we leave," I said.

"We can do whatever you want."

"I want to go see all the sights that people talk about. Oh, and I want to go to Milan! I looked everything up on Google, and I got a big ass list. You think they do the grape stomping like on *I Love Lucy* here?"

I turned over to look at him so he could see my excitement. Even in the dark, he was handsome to me. His bright, white teeth were almost glowing in the dark as he opened his mouth to laugh at me. I love this man so freaking much.

"We can do everything except the grape stomping. You are injured and I can't risk you getting hurt. As is you should still be resting and recovering," he said, and I pouted. He kissed my lips pulling me closer trying to make up for telling me no, but it wasn't working.

"Just say the word love and I can have them bring in a barrel and grapes for you to stomp at our home once you have healed. Or we could always fly out to Bordeaux, France."

"Why there?"

"It's the wine capital of the world, love." I just like how this man can make taking me to extravagant ass places sound like we just strolling up to Walmart, only Neron. I didn't have a response to that, so I figured it was best to change the topic.

"Tell me something about your childhood. I told you so many stories of me growing up. Stop hogging all the memories. I know your momma had you into some off the wall stuff." I laugh with him joining in.

"My mother was never really involved in our lives when we were kids. The staff pretty much raised my siblings and me. The only time mother would come around was for the debutante and beautillion balls she forced us to participate in. That and other public events were the rare times we spent together as a family. Other than that, she and my father stayed on their wing, and we stayed on ours. I was the fucked up of the family if you haven't noticed." He laughed, but I didn't.

"Fuck up how? You're a billionaire!" I snapped mad at his mama. Ion like that scatter edges, Bigen needing ass bitch for real now. Fucking with my man's feelings when he was a child. I should go fight her sad and boujie ass. Old, hoe. He sat up against the headboard in deep thought, like recalling the memories was hard for him.

"My parents had a guideline for us. Things that we were allowed to do and not allowed to do. My father was flexible, but mother wasn't. We could take whatever career paths we chose, but we had to be the absolute best. Princeton, Yale, Harvard, Brown, Penn State, Dartmouth, Columbia, and Cornell were the short list of college choices we were given. I chose MIT, yet to my mother even that was simply not enough. I chose to start my company from the ground up using money that I invested over the years, leaving my inheritance untouched. My mother felt that doing so was a foolish choice, saying that I could have used our family's name to have one of largest companies around. I have that now, but when I started, no one saw the vision that I saw. I knew my company wouldn't be what it is today, but to my family, I was just being Neron the fuck up. My mother never had faith in me, and to this day, she still questions my choices, but it doesn't sway me either way. I'm my own man, and I make the choices that I feel necessary."

I was hoping to get a funny memory, but I like this one all the same. It helps me understand him more. Neron is so driven, and at times he's like a machine. So, knowing what he just revealed, I see that it's because he's had to be everything for himself. He didn't have a strong support system, so he's had to push through on his own.

"Well, I know you're glad you took your own path," I replied, climbing my handicap ass on top of him.

Kissing and sucking on his neck, I swear he taste like a Hershey's kiss. His body is the chocolate I crave, and I'm addicted to his love. Kissing my way down his abs, I eased my good hand into his pants. His dick was rock hard and ready for everything I was about to do. Neron's was so swollen that my small hand could barely fit around him. Taking my tongue, I licked him from base to tip getting it nice and wet.

I let out a moan the more I sucked him because that shit was turning me in. Dick should never taste this good. My mouth was watering as I took him in and out. I heard the nigga's toes cracking, and he was doing his best not to moan, but the way my jaw locked around his thickness, he couldn't contain himself.

"Fuck! Just like that love!" he grunted, wrapping my weave up in his hands.

Looking up into his eyes as I sucked him up, I could see how good it felt, and that shit had my pussy leaking. Reaching out, he smacked me hard on the ass before using his long fingers to stir in my juice box. All that could be heard was the sweet symphony of our moans as we pleased one another. He had me squirting out, moaning, and drooling all over the dick. The excitement sent him off, and his sweet cum slid down my throat. He lifted me up and onto him so easily that my body took off again. I was on fire from the back-to-back releases. He started to slowly move in and out, and I couldn't take it!

"Wait! I can'ttttt!" I whined.

"You can and you will," he said in a cocky tone that had me purring. Daddy was hitting me with all the right moves.

Flipping me over, he took control pinning my legs back beating it down. You would have thought my pussy violated his G code the way he was fucking me. He fucked me silly until I passed out on his ass.

The next morning I woke up washed clean with breakfast lying in bed beside me. A bitch was on cloud nine, but my legs were on paraplegic. My ass couldn't walk for shit. He fucked me so good that my legs stopped working. This some shit I can have on the daily.

~

I leaned back on the boat admiring the buildings along the Grand Canal. I read on all the sites that seeing the Rialto Bridge was a must. So, on our last day, I pried Neron out of my pussy so we could see all the sights. I even wanted to try all the foods— from the pasta down to the pizza. Everything that this country is known for I want to try it and to see it. As we neared the bridge, I got my camera out, ready to take a thousand pictures. It was so fucking pretty that it took my breath away and tears stung my eyes.

I never thought I'd see something this damn beautiful and historic. I'm standing feet away from a place people dreamed of seeing. ME! Little Orphan Annie, Shantayla Rice. I just have to take this moment in. I felt Neron's hands wrap around me, grabbing the camera. He snapped the pictures that I was too caught up to get.

"The feeling that you have right now, that awestruck complete bewilderment, that is the feeling I have when I look at you. I get caught up looking into your eyes, like a moth to a flame. You trap me each time, love." His words made me blush.

"You always know just what to say to make me blush."

"I'm only speaking fact, love. Purely facts." With that, we stood looking out at the view together.

After the ride on the canal, he took me to all the restaurants. I'm not talking about the fancy shit. I went to the small family own restaurants where I knew the grandma was back in the kitchen fucking it up on the pots. I made the right decision too and ended up trying the best damn Ravioli and Seafood Risotto on the planet. I had her make two big pots of both, and I bagged them and put it in the freezer of the hotel. I wasn't leaving without having some to take home. I almost don't want to leave, but I know my girls need me back home. They're gone through some crazy shit.

NINE

Devon Gilbert

"I think we need to lay low for a while. Fame's been tailing me, and I think he might catch on," I said into the phone.

"I'll handle that; just have your ass over here tonight."

"Whatever, get off my line with that slick shit." I hung up before the caller could respond.

Fame is my nigga and my boss. The nigga pays me out the ass, and I'm thankful for everything he does for me. I got on with him through my big bro Gip. I was fresh out of Ju-Co with my trade degree in automotive, and I couldn't hold down a job for shit. I'm the best mechanic around, but most shop out this way is filled with too many slick mouthed niggas.

I kept fucking niggas up in every shop I was hired at. My big bro was fresh out the military working with Ice, and he put in the word to Fame about me. Me and that nigga hit it off instantly. He liked the fact that I never bowed down to any nigga. I'm a lay everybody down fuck the questions type of nigga, and he's rocking the same way.

The shit I've been on got me feeling fucked up. Knowing that I'm doing slick shit behind my nigga's back is fucking me up, but shit, I do what the fuck I want. When shit comes out, it comes out, and I'm forever standing behind my decisions. I pulled up to my bro's crib hopping out to head inside.

"GIP!" I called out. The nigga called me over here and ain't even up. I headed up the stairs and into his room, and the bitch was empty. This nigga is wasting my fucking time. I headed back out his crib and to my car. I got shit to fucking do; ian got time for this shit.

"Nigga, what the fuck?" I barked pulling my gun. Gip was sitting in the passenger seat of my ride when I got in. This nigga stays on creepy shit.

"You locked my door?"

"Yea."

"Let's ride out."

"To where nigga? You called me over not to take you nowhere."

"I just got to make a quick run to check some shit out. I put the GPS on" not bothering to respond. I let Siri guide me to South Dallas.

We pulled up outside a small run-down house, and Gip hopped out. I got out sitting on my hood pulling my fitted cap down just watching to see what the fuck he had going. This nigga snatched a broad out the house by her hair. The bitch was naked from the waist down with only a short t-shirt on. Ian gone lie her pussy was bald and pretty, and she got a fat ass.

"Bitch, where the fuck is my money?" he barked, sounding like he was pimping the hoe. I know better. Nine times out of ten the nigga was gone of the lean, and that bitch caught him slipping. Ion know why this nigga keeps fucking with that shit, knowing it knocks his ass out. I just sat back watching as he started smacking the bitch around with her screaming.

"It's in the house in my top drawer!"

With that, he tossed the bitch aside rushing into the house. He came back out heading back to my car. I hopped in cranking it up, and when he hopped in, I dig off.

"The fuck you call me out here for this dumb ass shit for nigga?"

"That bitch robbed me two weeks ago every time I pull in somebody warns the bitch. So, I needed you to roll up on her."

"How much she get you for?"

"Five hundred."

"Nigga, you're hurt over five hundred dollars? The Giuseppe's on yo feet more than that. You tripping."

"It's the principle. I can't have her out here thinking she can steal from me."

"You're slipping, bro. This ain't you right here," I said, and he shrugged.

He's been slipping further and further down the wrong road. Ever since my sis-in-law got sent upstate on an eight-year bid for a possessions charge. Gip was in Iraq at the time, and when he got the news, the nigga went AWOL trying to get to sis. When he got home, it wasn't shit he could do. She had already coped a plea taking the eight years. His commander looked out ofor him and gave him an honorable discharge when technically he was supposed to be court marshaled. When he got back home, he ain't want shit to do with the army or nothing else. Bro got up with Ice and Trouble and started hitting the streets. He's been on a downward spiral since.

One good thing I can say is that he can still get the job done. That nigga is Ice's right hand and never once has he dropped the ball, and that shit be shocking the fuck outta me cause he be leaning hard as fuck some nights. That's where that military shit pays off for his ass. It made him disciplined as fuck. Dropping him back off at his crib, I headed out to the shop. I've been there fixing up on cars on the side while laying low, shit.

~

"What you doing up here?" Vince asked, walking up to my station as I was lowering the car.

"Man, I been here since shit closed down. I thought yo ass would have been here too. What you been on?"

"I thought we were to lay low."

"On the hot shit, but it's still money to be made. Nigga, you be talking about your family gotta eat, but yeen acting like you trying to feed them."

I wasn't trying to clown the nigga but shit I always speak the truth. The nigga walks around the shop bigging up his family, but the minute shit gets hard, he ain't willing to go back to the small shit to feed his family 'til the heat dies down. That's flaw to me. Ian got no kids, and I been up here every day raking in the bread working on peoples' shit. It ain't 15K a pop, but the shit is still at around 2 to 3.

"I leave that to the help. It's suite you better than me after all." He smiled like the shit was a joke, but ian stupid.

"The fuck you say, muh'fucka," I said, walking up on him ready to lay his ass out. Just his luck, Fame rushed in saving the nigga.

"Cool it, Big Dee. We got some shit to handle."

I gave that nigga this one, but he'll never know when I pop up to get in his shit. I'll fuck around and show up at his doorstep to pistol whip his weak ass. Calling me the fucking help, nigga got life flipped all around.

"Arch and Gip are pulling two rides in. Vince, I need you on Gip's ride and Big Dee you get the one Arch rolling in. Use the presets I just taught y'all. I need that shit done quickly. Big Dee, are you done with this ride?"

"Yea she's done. I was gone paint it today, but that shit can wait."

"Nah, you good. I'll knock that shit out. It's been a minute since I fucked around with that shit," Fame said, heading towards his office.

"Aye Vince, you heard that?"

"The fuck you talking about?"

"I think they're calling yo number, fuckboy. Watch yo back."

"Is that a threat?" he retorted, making me laugh. This nigga is hilarious.

"I ain't ever seen a real nigga make threats. Everything I say is a hunnid. If you look in the mirror, you might see the grim reaper staring back. Ready to snatch yo life," I taunted, walking back to my station.

It was always something about the nigga that had me skeptical. Like I said he's always talking about his family and shit. If he wasn't talking about them then the nigga was quiet, but not the good quiet. He was quiet like he was up to something; he just comes off shady as fuck. He's good at his job, but he's weird. That shit and him slick talking got the nigga on my radar. Ion fuck with him just off that shit alone.

"What you tight for, nigga?" Gip said, getting out the car.

"Small shit. You waiting around?"

"Nah, I got some shit to handle. Arch gone sit it out."

"Cool," I said, dapping him and getting straight to business, taking the seats out and creating the small space I needed. The shit took all fucking day and into the night, but I ended up getting done first. Ion like taking breaks and shit like that. When I got work to do, I don't even fucking sleep until I get the shit done. That's just the workaholic in me.

"Aye yoo bro, come pick up the whip. I'm sitting here waiting for you."

"I'm on it." I hung up, waiting around on him. When he came, I handed the nigga the keys and headed out.

I'm tired as fuck, and all I want is some pussy and something to eat. A nigga was in heaven when I walked into my girl's crib, and she had breakfast waiting on a nigga. Shit like this makes me want to wife her ass. Most bitches would be down my throat about staying out all night without checking in, but she trusts a nigga. Or she's at least buttering me up to ask for something. Either way, I appreciate the meal.

"What happened to you coming over?" she asked, hugging me. I grabbed a hand full of her fat ass kissing her soft lips.

"I got caught up at the shop with Fame." Mentioning his name made her pull away.

"You didn't say anything, did you? We got a plan already in place I don't need you messing that up. What we got going is good, so don't fuck it up before time. Everything will fall into place in its own timing. Devon, don't mess it up feeling guilty. You're doing what's best for us."

"What I look like snitching, that shit ain't even in me. The shit is already done now, ain't no coming back from this shit. At this point, all we can do is go forward with the plan." Satisfied with my response, she kissed me again.

I was ready to slide up into her, but I'm dirty as fuck from the shop. I'm tearing that pussy up after I filled my stomach and washed my nuts. She gone have to beg me to come out that sweet pussy she got. Smacking her on the ass, I followed behind her into the kitchen. I washed up and sat down to eat breakfast. Every now and then I'd look up at her. I stole one last glanced and smirked at how I'm risking everything over some pussy. Rookie mistake, but it is some bomb ass pussy though.

TEN

Lai

Creeping out of bed, I walked to the stairs heading over to the only corner that is out of the camera's range. Trouble thinks I don't know that he has cameras all over, but I cleaned this place from top to bottom. I know where 85% of his things are hidden. Slipping into the corner, I pulled out my phone from behind a loose brick in the wall. I scrolled through my messages, laughing at Shanty and Niyah's texts before going to the one I was most curious about.

Jacob: Can you meet me later today?

Me: I can try

Jacob: I really just need to talk to someone. Everything is just fucked up right now. I really wish my sister were here. She was always there to listen.

Me: I'll come by the apartment in the morning.

I quickly put the phone away because I could hear the stairs creak. I ran to the kitchen, pretending to drink a glass of water. I couldn't hear him, but I knew he was behind me. I could just feel him there. With a quick yank of my hair, he exposed my neck to bite me, driving me crazy. As he bit and sucked on my spot, his hand snaked under my nightgown and into my panties. My back arched as my hips danced in sync with his magical fingers.

"Ohhhh!" I moaned as his finger toyed with my clit, fluttering back and forth like hummingbird wings. He skillfully worked me into an orgasm as my mouth hung open letting my pleasures escape. Before I could come down, he ripped my panties off, entering me from behind. With his hand on the back of my neck pushing me down, he pounded into me. His strokes were so deep and powerful that our skin clapped together, echoing through the room.

"Take this dick!" he grunted smacking my ass repeatedly as I moaned out. "Yea! Tell me how that dick feel?"

"IT'S SOOOO GOOOD! Shit! Fuck me harder!"

Obeying my wishes, he turned me around putting my legs over his shoulders and fucked me so hard that I was leaking like a hot mixtape. I was doing my best to use my hands to push him back because the pressure was too intense, but he wasn't letting up.

"Stop running!" he barked, pushing my hands aside. He continued to bounce me up and down on his thickness. I clamped down around him as I came hard and fast. He grunted, thrusting into me quickly before I felt his dick twitch. I wrapped my arms around his neck as he carried me to the bed.

"We not done just yet," he said, laying me down slow grinding into me. He had my mind gone as he fucked me for hours until we both passed out from exhaustion.

~

I woke up at a little before nine and Trouble was still asleep. I eased into the shower quickly, making sure to keep the noise to a minimum. I threw on some sweat, grabbed my hidden cell, and walked down the street to catch my Uber. I know of a fact Trouble has a tracker on everything that's why I haven't told him about my cell phone. He's so controlling that he always has to know where I am and what I'm doing. I made it to my old apartment in under an hour, and Jacob was inside waiting for me. The place was a mess. I know that Jacob is having a rough time, but he is a fucking slob.

"Jacob, you could at least clean."

I began picking up old beer bottles and food packaging. I have been taking care of him since he I got back in contact with him three weeks ago. I put money into his account and try to make sure he has what he needs. It's hard to do with Trouble being so involved in my every move, but I've been managing to make it work.

"I'm working on it." His words came off in a slur, causing me to look at him.

"You're high JACOB!"

"I just need to take the edge off. It's been hard lately."

"BULLSHIT! You can't keep doing this. You said you were quitting cold turkey."

"I'm trying. I'm here all alone and all think about is my sister. Maybe if we go away somewhere together, then you could help me. I need someone, Lai."

"I will see Jacob. I have to go, but I'll be back tomorrow. Just try to stay clean until then. Please!" I begged, hugging him close to me. He was the closest thing I could get to having Sheila back, and I feel responsible for making sure he survives. I can't let him ruin his life.

"Ok." With that, I cleaned the house back up and cooked him breakfast before leaving.

I called Mama Rosemary telling her that I was on my way over in case Trouble was looking for me. I told her that sometimes I like to go to the park to write and get some fresh air so she covers for me with Trouble. I honestly think she does it because she knows how he can get. I still haven't figured out if he's still seeing that woman or not. I know he hasn't come home smelling of her anymore, but that's not to say he doesn't still communicate with her. All know is I know how to handle him and her the next time it happens.

"Malaika Coleman," a deep voice called from behind me as I walked to my Uber. I turned to see a handsome older man. His voice was faintly familiar, but I couldn't place it.

"Oh, you don't remember me? I'm former Detective Markus Stringer, the man who wanted to nail your ass to the cross for being complicit in two murders. That was until your parents ruined mine and my partner's careers. Add him to your list of victims because he drank himself to death." His words stung harder than his bitter tone.

"It's all almost worth it to see that look on your face. You know I was going to kill you, but instead, I'll leave you with this." He handed me a large thick envelope before walking off.

Putting the envelope aside, I got into my Uber and headed to Mama Rosemary's home. I can open it when I get there. The last thing I need is for Trouble to wake up searching for me and I'm not where I said I would be.

I've already been out for almost three hours I can't see him sleeping in any later than noon. Pulling into the driveway, I spotted an all black Camaro. Seeing that she had company, I took the opportunity to open the envelop while sitting on the swing seat on her porch. The envelop was filled with files and photos. Carefully slipping everything out I looked over them with tears of hurt and sadness filling my eyes.

It was crime scene photos, incident reports, and other documents. All from people whom I've either directly hurt, or were hurt in the fall out of my actions. I could stomach looked at Sheila's body slumped over in the passenger seat of my dad's totaled car. Her eyes were still opened. Tears slid down one by one as I touched the picture of my best friend. They had of pictures of Melissa sitting on the table in the morgue. You could see the discoloration from the bruises the rope left. It pained me to look, but I couldn't turn away. I slowly thumbed through it all.

Melissa parents filed for divorce two months after her funeral. Her younger brother ran away; there are several files of his arrest, and one is DOC paper. He's in prison for 20 years for armed robbery. On the comment section, they included his arresting officer's notes *"Attempted suicide by cop, must be placed on strict suicide watch"*. They have him in the psychiatric facility serving his full sentence.

Detective Stinger's partner had two kids and a wife. After he lost his job and drank himself to death, he lost his pension. Her check stubs and receipts were photocopied in the file. She works two jobs to barely pay for the cheap motel the three of them live in. Tossing the photos aside, they flew all over as the slight breeze carrying some into the yard. I let out a loud cry praying that I could scream away the agonizing guilt. I fucked up so many people's lives in just two days.

"Who the fuck is out here with all that noise?" Mary Rosemary shouted, rushing out with her gun drawn. Seeing me, she tucked it in the small of her back before sitting next to me on the swing. She pulled me in wrapping her arms around me, just letting me cry on her shoulder.

"What is all these papers over my yard?"

"It's all my fault. I'm the reason all their lives are fucked up!" I screamed harder with her hugging me tighter.

"I don't know what happened, and I don't need to know. All I know is that guilt is a silent killer. You keep hanging on to all that mess," she said, pointing to the papers scattered around. "Then you never be able to make it right. If you feel like it was your fault, own up to it and do what you have to make right what you can. The things that you can't make right, accept that as the consequences of life. We all fuck up, sometimes intentionally, but that's not what should define you. Stop hanging on to that and be better than who you were when you did all that." I nodded my head and hugged back.

"Come on, I'm cooking and Donavan on his way over." As we walked inside a guy was heading out.

"Isn't that—"

"I kept your secrets and now keep mine. Don't mention that," she said, causing me to laugh. I shrugged it off, and we headed inside.

I talked with her until Trouble came giving me a death stare, but he knew better than to say anything to me in front of his mom. She'll fuck him up, with the quickness. I just sat back thinking of what Mama Rosemary said, and I knew that I had to help Jacob get sober. It's the only way I can make right with him for Sheila's death. I've made up my mind that I'm finding a way to sneak off with Jacob. I have to help him get clean, and if that's the only way, I'm going to do it.

ELEVEN

Fame

"How do you know when a woman knows something?" Trouble asked from beside me as we sat in my shop. I was rebuilding an engine for a customer, and I barely heard him cause I was thinking about Big Dee. That nigga is hiding something, and I know it. I consider that nigga a brother, but I don't believe in coincidences. Somebody is sabotaging my business at the same time he's acting weird. It's all too close for comfort. My first mind is telling me to kill the nigga, but I'm maturing and all that shit, so I figured I should get answers first.

"Nigga, I don't fucking know. Women are psychics they know shit that they ain't even supposed to know. You can fuck a bitch's in yo dreams, and they'll find out. If you think she knows bro, then she definitely knows something. Why?"

"Lai's been acting sneaky lately. Then she's been dropping hints and shit."

"Hints to what?"

"I fucked that old bitch one day when Lai was getting on my fucking nerves."

"Nigga, you just do crazy shit. All that talking to me about Shanty and you go and fuck a broad that's three days from wearing depends. If Lai doesn't know, she will when Debbie's old ass gets word about you and her. You've been fucking around with that old hoe too long to let her go out shame. Bro, I promise she gone start up some shit. Then, watch how Niyah and Shanty have Lai acting."

"That old bitch knows her place."

"Said all the other niggas that got caught slipping. Nigga, these side bitches ain't got no code of honor. They be straight out here trying to get a nigga by any means necessary. You fucked up, bro. You might as well get ready for the blowback."

"Lai, ain't like that." I just looked at him. I'm convinced this nigga got a mental issue; it's like the nigga is missing some links.

"The fuck you mean she ain't like that. Nigga ALL women are like that. It's a Chinese broad across the waters right now chopping a nigga dick off to serve it up in some stir-fry. Nigga, keep sleeping on Lai talking about what she ain't like and you gone be hiding in the bushes at her new nigga's mansion.

Ian been to sleep since Shanty left my ass. Bro, I ain't even touched a bitch. I ordered a bad bitch deluxe from the Adam&Eve site. I'll go home and wear that blow-up doll out, but ian fucking no bitch, period. If it ain't Shanty, my dick don't even twitch. Her marrying that nigga fuck me up bad. Leave Debbie's old dusty pussy ass alone."

"I hear you, bro."

Ion think he really did, but that ain't my problem. When Lai gets in his shit, that's on him. Shit, I got plenty scars and bruises for fucking off on Shanty. Every time she caught me with a bitch, she was on my ass. I took that shit as a joke back then, but now I see that how I was acting was fucked up. She held me down, and ion think another bitch can love me as hard as she did.

That's why I'm solo dolo, fuck these bitches. I done had enough pussy to last a lifetime, so ian missing shit by falling back. I finished chopping it up with Trouble about his shit before I headed out for the day. It's one o'clock in the afternoon, but I been up since yesterday. As soon as I got out the shower, it hit the bed hard.

"Fame, Fame, Fameeeeee!" I heard Shanty's voice, but it was too melodic. Like when a ghost calls you in the movies. A nigga was scared to open my eyes.

"Is this how you like it, daddy?"

Now that shit popped my eyes right open. I like it any way she's giving it. Looking at her, my dick stood up straight. She had on a black lingerie set with some sexy sheer pantyhose. Her breasts sat up perfectly, looking like ripe melons. She has a flat stomach with thick hips and thighs, giving her the perfect hourglass figure. Shanty got the sexiest body I've ever seen; my shawty is bad.

"Get it ready for me," she purred.

I wet my hand quickly and started slowly jacking my dick. I watched as she twirled around bending over to give me a view of that fat ass. Slipping her panties off, she spread her ass for me letting me see inside her pussy. My mouth watered, looking at her slip her finger into her wet box.

"Get that shit wet and nasty for daddy."

Doing as I said, she took her hands from her pussy sticking them in her mouth getting them wet before rubbing them back around mixing it with her juices. That shit had pre-cum oozing from my shit. I love when my bitch gets nasty.

"Bring me some pussy. I'm tired of playing."

She came over, and I picked her up sitting her on my face going in on that pussy. Using my tongue to spread her lips and suck the juices straight out of her juice box, I was licking and slurping my way to her soul. Shanty's pussy got my head gone.

"Eat it, daddy," she purred, causing me to smack her on the ass.

Flicking my tongue on her clit, I had her juices leaking like a broken dam. Slurping it all up, I flipped her over and slid right into her working my way around her tight walls slowly stroking her, hitting her sweet spot, making her scream out my name. Over and over I hit her spot, feeling her legs get weaker with each thrust. I want to give her a nut that she'll never forget.

"Who's pussy is this?" I moaned, nibbling on her ear.

"It's yours! It's all yours."

I grabbed both of her ankles putting them together making her knees touch her forehead and went in, straight homicidal in the pussy. With her ass screaming and bucking harder than ever as that pussy clamped down around me, I bite my lip to muffle the bitch ass moans that were threatening as I came long and hard.

"I love you, Fame!"

My doorbell rang waking me up before I could tell her I loved her back. Hopping up, I had nut everywhere. Whoever was at my door gone have to wait until I wash up. I handled my hygiene quick and headed for the door. Vince was posted up against the wall outside the front entrance.

"What's happening?" I said slapping hands with him.

"We got another call. I think this time it's quite obvious who is the culprit. Luckily, it was only a gun in the hidden compartment under the seat," he said, and I nodded heading into the living room. I sat on the sofa giving the shit time to permeate. I'm pissed that I didn't off the nigga off the top.

"Which car was it?"

"It was the all black Mustang that I worked on." That piqued my interest, and I already knew what was up.

"Keep yo eye out on him for me. Hit him up and tell him what happened. Get the car to us, holler at ole boy at the holding yard and he'll let it go with no hassle. We don't have time to wait for the auction with this one. I want that nigga to lie to me in my face so that I can lay him down right then and there. I've been more than generous. When I eat we all eat, the fuck can a nigga get out of crossing me. That's some greedy shit." I caught the look he gave me, but ian say shit. This shit fucking with everybody's heads.

"Well, I have to go. My daughter has a soccer game." I got up with him following him to the door. I stood out front, watched this nigga climb into a red Ferrari, and chuckled to myself heading back inside.

~

I stepped out of my ride and walked up to Big Dee's condo, walking straight in not bothering to knock. Pouring a glass of Henny from his mini bar I took a seat on his couch lighting my blunt. I was making myself real comfortable in this bitch. Shit, after all, I may have to sell this shit to get my bread back. I figured he had a woman in the back because I smelled a familiar floral scent. It was a mature scent; something like the shit Mama Rosemary would wear. Shrugging it off, I threw the drink back and made another. I was good and lifted by the time the nigga walked in from the back.

"Yo, who the fuck in my shit?" he barked, upping his pistol on me. I chuckled and exhaled my smoke blowing O's to be funny with the nigga.

"Put that shit down and come talk to me, homie."

"Fame, nigga, we cool and all, but don't be popping up to my shit unannounced like that," he said with authority, but that shit wasn't moving me.

"You know why they call me Fame?" I asked still blowing O's.

"Cause you a pretty boy ass nigga that like to shine or some shit like that." He sat down on the couch opposite of me. The nigga was still tight, but that shit didn't faze me none.

"Nawl, Mama Rosemary used to always quote this saying 'Fame knows no bounds'. She started referring to me as Fame cause I go where I want to go and do what the fuck I want to do."

"Nigga, what the fuck is yo problem. I think you finally lost yo fucking mind."

"Nah, I'm just chilling and thinking. Vince came up to the shop today to tell me that one of the two cars you two niggas worked on got hit. That's three so far. My record is shot out here. No nigga is gone come to me for shit now. That's ain't even the craziest part, Dee," I said, laughing and sitting upright. "Vince thinks that it's you that's giving away my presets."

"Fam, you know me well enough to know ion got no reason to be on no fuck shit like that."

"Who knows, you've been real shifty lately, homie. You ain't looked me in the eyes in months. Shid, if you ask me your body language is telling a story of its own. That shit is screaming 'FRAUD ALERT, FRAUD ALERT!'. Tightening up Big Dee, I heard they catching niggas slipping. Be at the shop tomorrow night at 8, don't be late," I said before standing up and walking out the door.

I grabbed the bottle of Hennessy I was drinking from, taking it to go. I'm trying to amp up my dreams of Shanty. I know if I'm gone off that Henn shit will get even freakier. I'm trying to get to pin her ass upside down and eat that pussy while she's sucking all this dick. Shid, maybe "dream Shanty" will let me bring a bad bitch in so we can all have fun.

Thinking about her ass made me drive past her job. I know Shanty well enough to know that she wasn't quitting her job, even if she is married to that Bill Gates ass nigga. I sat outside for a good hour waiting on her. When she walked out her arm was in a sling but other than that, she was perfect. She had her hair pulled up in a bun making her cheeks stand out. Her chocolate skin seemed to glow underneath the sunlight. My body reacted automatically to the sway of her hips under the fabric of her pencil skirt.

I'm the type of nigga that loves seeing a woman in heels. The way they accentuate the flow of the hips is fucking mind-blowing. Shanty had on a pair of black red bottoms, and she was walking off like she was on the runway. Everything about her seemed so different as if she had more life in her. My pride took a tumbling when I saw that nigga walk up and pull her into his arms. The way she reacted to him pissed me off, and I got that crazy feeling I had when I shot her ass. Cranking up my car, I drove off fast as fuck. If I didn't, I would end up killing them both. Shit was hitting me all over again because I fucking lost the love of my life. All I got now is my dreams of us together.

TWELVE

Niyah

I sat up against my headboard finsihing up on *Trapped by This Thing Called Love* by T. Smith, trying my best not to lose my mind. If it weren't for my Kindle, I swear I'd be bat shit crazy right now. Ice got me living like a fucking prisoner in this big ass house. Shit, at least when Lai was a house bitch Trouble talked to her ass. Ice walks around this bitch like I don't exist.

I could be staring straight in his face, and he'd look right through me. Ian never been an insecure bitch, but something telling me he's entertaining a bitch. I'm a damn stripper, so I know what niggas do when shit is going bad on the home front. The only thing that's slightly easing my troubled mind is the fact that I heard Ice say Andre is dead. That shit was a big relief off me because it meant that my son ain't in danger.

Putting my Kindle down, I sat up looking around. I'm horny, bored, and frustrated. I been reading nothing but urban fiction since I've been on lockdown. Do you know how frustrating shit is when you reading about bitches getting fucked and you ain't getting none? Shit is sad. My fingers should be stuck up my pussy with how much I been caressing my walls.

Fuck this shit. I'm about to rape this nigga and ian playing. Slipping out of all my clothes, I eased out of the room tiptoeing to his. Opening his door, I realized that he wasn't in bed, so I made my way to his office. The light was on so I knew he was probably working, Ice is the definition of a workaholic. Barging through the door, I step in naked and proud. It wasn't until I caught three sets of eyes on me that I realized he had company.

"Niyah, what the fuck?" Ice shouted. Gip and Archie hurriedly turned their head, but I caught Archie staring at my pussy for a second too long.

"Are you gone come fuck me or not?" I asked not budging or trying to cover up.

"GET THE FUCK OUT!" he barked, but it wasn't moving me. Dick is the only thing that's getting me up outta here.

"So, is that a no?"

Out of nowhere, he hopped up snatching me up by my hair dragging me out of the room. His grip was so tight on my hair that I thought it would detach from my scalp.

"You're hurting me!" All of my cries went unheard as he pulled into his bedroom, releasing my hair with a hard push.

"You want some dick?" he asked as he freed his pants.

"Come suck my fucking dick and you better not choke," he gritted, pulling me up by my hair sending more pain to my tingling scalp.

Sucking back all the emotions and taking my cue, I approached the mic ready to rock it just right! Slowly licking him from base to tip paying close attention to the head, I flicked my tongue back and forth around it making his dick twitch in my hands. Sucking him all in with my wet, tight mouth, I bobbed on his tool, looking him directly in the eyes.

"GRRRR!" he grunted, grabbing my hair tighter.

Taking both hands, I stroked him opposite directions while tightening my mouth more to suck him in deeper. The sensation made him thrust deeper into my mouth, and I relaxed my throat letting him sink inside.

"Gag on that shit!" he demanded, thrusting harder into my mouth.

Slipping my tongue out, I let him go as deep as I could, taking more of him in. Tears stung my eyes ass I gagged on his big dick. Grabbing my head, he took over thrusting in and out causing me to gag and slob like crazy. I removed my hands and started playing with my pussy. I threw my head back removing him from my mouth completely.

"Play in that pretty pussy and let me see it."

With one hand, I grabbed his dick and with the other, I fingered my pussy giving him a good show. I eased his head back into my mouth and sucked it before popping it out, making his dick twitch and expand. He was ready to buss. I eased him back in and teased his head more, licking and sucking it just right before taking him deep in the back of my throat where he came long and hard. At the same time, I was hitting my spot and creaming all over the floor. Before I could even react, he was snatching me to my feet.

"Don't fucking playing with me, Ni! I will fucking kill you if you try that shit again. When my door is closed, knock on that shit. Clean this shit up and get in the fucking bed!" he demanded, putting his dick in his pants and walking out.

I should be mad, but sucking dick is still better than not even getting to touch the dick, and a bitch got a nut in so I can't complain. I cleaned the mess up and laid my happy ass right in his bed. He can say what he wants, but I'm sleeping in this damn room. I might roll over and slip on the dick in the middle of the night too. This ain't no Trouble and Malaika; I will not play happy hostage for nothing. Ion care if I was plotting against him. Ignacio got shit fucked up.

~

I talked all that shit about Malaika and guess what the fuck I'm doing? This nigga got me in here cleaning and cooking meals and shit. I swear somebody in hell is drinking a big ass glass of ice water right now. This goes to show you that my ass is thirsty for the dick. All he did was let me taste it, and I'm already back in la la land. Turning on old-school slow jams' playlist, I started on the laundry.

All there was, was our lounge clothes cause Ice takes his other clothes to the cleaners.

After loading the clothes, I washed the few dishes and started my meatloaf. This nigga is getting meatloaf, potatoes, and steamed green beans. If that's not good enough, he may as well call Greta's old ass back so she can hook him up with the usual. My phone started to ring as I was peeling the potatoes. I set the shit down cleaning my hands to pick it up.

"Hello?"

The caller remained silence, making me repeat myself with a nasty attitude. Ian got time for this shit, not today. I'm up in this bitch playing Florida Evans waiting on James' ass. I'll fuck around and smash a plate hollering DAMN! DAMN! DAMN!

"Whoever the fuck this is go lick the dirt outcha great-grand-mamma dead ass pussy instead of fucking playing with me. I hope yo phone short circuit and burn yo ear off dumb ass bitch!" I spat about to hang up until I heard a deep voice laughing.

"That pussy was real pretty last night."

I looked at the phone, trying to make sure my ears were hearing me right. Cause I know good and well this nigga didn't call my gah damn phone talking about my pussy.

"Thank you, goodbye!"

"Hang up, and that's your son's life."

"What the fuck do you mean? How do you have my baby?" My nerves instantly got the best of me, and I was breaking down. Just when I thought Andre's death meant Anju was safe, I was wrong.

"That's not for you to worry about. Andre's death doesn't stop the plans. No matter where your son is, we can still get to him. Think about that and be waiting on my call," the caller said before hanging up.

I fell back into my chair just staring at my hands crying my eyes out. I'm stuck between a rock and a hard place once again, where it's either my life or my son's. I love Ice I truly do, but how could I ever risk my son's life. Trust is what he keeps preaching to me, but how can I trust my son's life with a man who isn't his father.

If his father didn't want him, what the hell would make me

think that Ice could want him. Looking at the time, I put my game face on and finished cooking. The whole time my mind was going back and forth between telling Ice and trusting that he could keep Anju safe wherever my parents are him hiding or just keeping things to myself in hopes that everything would be okay.

I was so deep in my thoughts that my body was on autopilot simply performing the tasks at hand not giving them much thought as I pondered my decision. This was literally some life or death shit, and it's weighing heavily on me. I didn't even notice Ice had walked into the house until I turned taking the plates to the table. He scared the shit out of me, and I almost dropped the food.

"Why didn't you say anything?"

"I did, you ain't answer back. Sit the plates down for a minute. I gotta talk to you." My heart started pounding, and I clutched the plates tighter as he tried to take them to sit them on the island. Realizing what I was doing, I released them. He sat on a stool, pulling me between his legs. The way he was staring into my eyes took away all my anxiety. I don't know what it is, but we connect, even when we are at odds we got a strong connection. One so strong that people in the room with us can feel it.

"Before you say what you have to say I have something to tell you," I said, fighting back the tears. My mind was telling me not to do it, that it was too big of a risk, but my heart, my heart was screaming for me to pour it all out and just trust in him.

"Ignacio, this is so hard, and I'm so fucking scared." Tears slipped from my eyes as I mustered up the courage to get it all out. "I got a call today saying that the plan is still on and that my sons will always be in danger no matter where he is. I wanted so bad not to tell you, but I trust you to keep him safe. Please find my baby and keep him safe." I burst into tears, and he pulled me close hugging me tightly. He stood to his feet lifting me off the ground, and I wrapped my legs around him continuing to cry into his neck.

"I got something for you, Ni. Open your eyes," he said gently tapping my thigh. Reluctantly, I turned to look at the door just as it was opening and Anju was rushing inside. I couldn't get out of Ice's arms quick enough to catch my son. He was so freaking big.

"Mama." All I could do was pull him close to me and sob. Happy, was even the word to express this feeling. Having my son back is everything. Standing up holding my seven-year-old son like he was a toddler I rushed to Ice clutching him for dear life.

"I love you so much," I cried as I held onto him and my son.

"Aye, we gone holla at y'all later," a familiar voice, said I turned around to see Gip and Archie, standing at the door.

"Okay see you guys later," I said, rushing them out the door.

When they left, I rushed over locking the door. I grabbed Ice's hand still holding Anju like an oversized baby as I lead us all to the backyard so we wouldn't be heard. Ain't no telling if they bugged the house. Putting Anju down, I let him run around the big open space.

"Thank you so much for getting him back, babe. I'm can never express it enough. I hate to ruin our moment, but you got a fraud ass nigga on your team!" I blurted out, and he turned bright red. I told him all about the call, and he nodded his head, leaving out making sure to lock the door promising to send Lai over. I was scared, but I also know that this is what he has to do in order to keep Anju and me safe. He gotta get the snakes out of his garden.

THIRTEEN

Ice

I've been working nonstop with Gip to get shit in order concerning Anju. As soon as I put him on the job, he got Ni's parents call logs and bank statements. That shit paid off because in 5 days he had locations, one by one we checked them all out, and we found him. They had him ducked off in a gated community in Grapevine. One ride through and we saw him out front playing with an older Korean lady. She looked just like Ni, so I figured she was her grams. I put someone on the house while I went downtown to straighten shit out.

Imagine my surprise when I found out her parents never had custody of her son. That shit was all a ploy to control Ni. All it took to shut that shit down was one visit letting them know I knew what was up. They handed lil dude right over. Of course, they made call down to the station, but shit, as a part of The Camp, my pull down there is just as long as theres. Wasn't shit to be said to me or Ni about getting him back. They took him on some fraud shit, and when shit settles, I'm gone see them about fucking over Ni like that, that's my word.

Hearing Ni tell me one of my niggas was a snake fucked me up. I mean a nigga is taking more Ls than I can fucking count right now. Two broads and now one of my right-hand men. This some urban fiction, shit. A nigga in real life can't be this fucking unlucky. Hopping in my ride, I headed straight for Trouble's crib, hitting up Fame to meet me there.

If I can't trust anybody, I know that I can fucking trust my brothers no matter what. I got up the street and decided to turn back. Right now ion even trust them being out of my sight. I ran in, scooped them up, and headed back out. Lil dude was knocked out in Ni's arm. I can't get over how she is holding him like he's a six-month-old baby. She's definitely cherishing her moment and ian mad at her.

"You need me to get him for you?"

"I got him. I'm good." The rush in her tone let me know she was feeling some type of way about that call.

I need to get this shit handled sooner than letter cause I can't have dysfunction in my home. Even though I'm still pissed at her, I gotta make sure she and lil dude are safe and worry-free. That's my job as the man of the household. I pulled up to Trouble's crib and headed inside. I didn't even bother knocking on the door cause the nigga knew I was coming. We walked into him and Lai going at it down in his dungeon. I couldn't hear what they were saying, but Trouble voice carried heavy, and she sounded like a squeaky mouse responding.

"Bitch, go lay down or something before I knock you the fuck out!" he barked, storming up the stairs.

Lai came up behind him throwing something at his ass, and he turned around smacking her hard as hell. I hopped up, pulling him back before he did some damage.

"Move!" Trouble barked, staring a hole at Lai who hopped up looking scared as fuck.

"Can y'all cool all that down? My son is sleep," Ni said in a hard whisper.

"Ni, take Lai and y'all go out to Mama Rosemary's. Don't stop or do shit but go straight there. Somebody will be there when y'all make it. Don't fucking stop for shit, Ni."

"Ok!" she snapped back, rushing out the door with Lai hot on her heels.

"That bitch is being sneaky!" Trouble roared.

It wasn't that I didn't care it's just that his relationship shit would have to take the back burner. I got more important shit that we got to talk about.

"Bro, cool it on that shit. Go take a shot and calm your nerves. We got important shit to hash out, right now."

"Only shit I'm taking is to that bitch's dome."

I was happy as fuck when Fame walked through the door. Cause I wasn't about to talk to that nigga bout this shit. If he says he wants to kill her ass, nine out of ten times he'll fuck around and do it. Ion want no part of they relationship drama, just like he don't want any of mine.

"Nigga, I hear you from outside that steel door. The fuck you barking about?"

"I'm gone kill that sneaky little bitch."

"Nigga, you started that shit. Ice, what's up bro? I got some shit to handle at the shop."

"Y'all know Ni was getting blackmailed by that nigga Andre. Well, Archie told me that the nigga clocked out, but today Ni got a call threatening her again. This time they mentioned some shit that happened last night when only Gip and Arch was at the crib. "

"So, one of them is in on the shit, too?" Fame asked.

"Most definitely, and I already know who."

"Aye, come ride out with me on this shit. I got a feeling everything is about to start making sense. I told you in that car when we were watching Ali that shit seemed to all tie in." I nodded at what Fame said, and we all got up hopping into Trouble's truck heading to Fame's shop.

We pulled up to the shop, and Big Dee and Vince were already there. I peeped the Ferrari parked, and I looked back at Fame curiously. I know Fame got long money and his niggas are paid too, but gah damn. Niggas driving Ferrari in the hood now, that's some flashy shit. Walking inside, we heard Big Dee and Vince going at it. Luckily, we rushed in before Big Dee pulled the trigger. He was about to blow Vince's shit back.

"CHILL!" Fame barked. Big Dee looked back like he was considering saying fuck it and just off the nigga, but he thought better and lowered his gun.

"The fuck going on?"

"He's a snake boss. He came in here threatening my life if I didn't go along with his crazy plan," Vince ranted, spewing blood as he snitched like a bitch. Off that alone, I wouldn't trust shit he had to say. It's not what he said it's the fucking way he said it. That shit came out too easily like he already had that shit lined up.

"Yo, believe all that heat he spitting if you choose, but I'm always a hunnid how I carry mines. It ain't no hoe in me period. The fuck I look like leveraging this bitch ass nigga?" Big Dee spat.

"Yo V, you know what's tripping me out?" Fame asked rhetorically before laughing and throwing the keys to Dee. "Go over there and used the preset I just showed you on that Mustang."

He mugged Vince and went to the car. He cranked it up before doing some extra shit, then turning it back off and doing it all over again.

"It doesn't work," he responded, and the color washed from Vince's face. The nigga realized that he fucked up.

"I never gave the two of you the same presets. So, look I'm gone cut to the chase and just give you the time to fill us the fuck in because ian got time to fuck around," Fame said, cocking his gun.

"I had no choice," he cried like a female, and I looked at Trouble at the same times as he looked at me.

"Shid, that Ferrari outside is showing a lot of options," Trouble commented. Fame got hot and shot the nigga in the right thigh, sending him to the ground quick.

"HURRY THE FUCK UP!" There's that hot-headed shit. That nigga is gone kill him before we figure out what the fuck is up. Vince was clutching his leg rolling around crying out in pain.

"3, 2—" This nigga was shooting the nigga as he counted.

Starting at the other leg moving up to his arms. I guess the nigga got the good sense he need to talk before Fame hit one

"I was there when you had nothing. Me! I worked hard to help you build this and for what. Shop Manager! I deserve to be partner!"

Without hesitation, Fame shot his ass in the left shoulder. That shit caused him to go back on his screaming and moaning shit. The nigga was acting like a straight up bitch. I've seen niggas take six or seven shots and still keep going. This nigga was dying with no honor. His ass better stop fucking around cause he ain't got no more limbs, all that left is the head shot.

"I don't give a fuck about yo fucking feelings. Do I look like Dr. Phil or Oprah and shit? I don't care about none of that fuck shit. The fuck I'mma make you partner for when I fronted everything for this shit. Yea, you got a manager position, but I pay you fucking double. Get to the fucking point of this shit cause I'm bored already."

"I got approached by an old cop, Markus Stinger. He runs a criminal enterprise now, and he offered me a half a mil to turn on you. I took it happily. Hell, I would have done it for free," he said, and Fame sent a bullet to his head. I just knew this nigga was gone do that shit before we finished getting answers.

"Bro, how the fuck we gone get answers if you killed the motherfucker?" Trouble shouted.

"Fuck this nigga! He ain't got the answers we need. He told us who was running shit. Let's get the information from the horse's mouth. You niggas want to sit around playing patty cake and braid in the nigga's hair then do that, but ian got time to be torturing niggas for information and only get half the fucking plot. I want all my information at once.

Big Dee, you got three days to get at me about whatever the fuck you been hiding, bro. Three days from this moment, or I'm popping up and sending you to join that nigga!" Fame spat, giving him the order to call clean up as we walk out the door.

"Bro, I called y'all to handle my shit. How the fuck we get

dragged into yours. I still got one of my niggas out to get my family."

"Bro, it ain't hard to know that Archie's the one on that snake shit. Gip and Big Dee are some loyal niggas, they may have they secrets, but they ain't bitch made. Archie's the type that want to be more than what he is. I peeped that shit long ago, but he's yo peoples," Trouble said.

"Pull up on his crib. Let's follow that nigga."

"Here you go with this bullshit, bro. Just kill the nigga and let's see about this nigga Markus. I told you I hate this pussyfooting shit." Fame snapped.

"Nah, we gone follow him and let Ni feed them information. If we play shit cool, we can catch them all up," I said with Trouble nodding. Sometimes you gotta play dumb in order to get to what it is you really want. It's more to this shit than we all know, and I think it makes more sense to let him lead us to them all instead of going after everybody one by one.

FOURTEEN

Markus

Seeing the look on that bitch Malaika's face when I revealed myself made my dick hard. Knowing that she is consumed with guilt is better than death, especially after my parting gift. Those pictures and files will torment her for the rest of her life. I wanted to murder her, but seeing that she was with Trouble, I knew that I couldn't get near her. It's bad enough that I have to kill his brothers. Going near her will lead him straight to me. It's no secret her family ruined my life, but my ties with his brothers is a secret only I hold. Trouble is a man who can make things difficult for me.

I could lie and say that I'm not skeptical about killing them too, but I am. They are proving to be smarter than I estimated. I chose Ice first because he seemed to be the lesser threat. It's no secret that Fame is a careless hot head. Some think that it's a flaw, but in actuality, it makes him harder to target. It's harder to pinpoint a vulnerability to exploit.

Well, that was until I realized that his worker Vince was trying to start his own shop under Fame's nose. He came straight to me offering to provide cars for my runs free of charge if I loaned him the startup money. It was a great proposition, but I had a better one. He agreed to help me ruin Fame's business, and I already had my brother working to destroy Ice. A knock on the door jarred me from my thoughts.

"Come in," the quiet one I put in charge, Archie, walked in with the two dumbasses.

"We got some issues," Archie said.

I sat back in my seat observing the remaining three on my team, and I had to chuckle. I must be a weak ass boss cause two out of the three are fucking jokes. One is going through withdrawals so bad that he's doing the two-step, and the other is talking to himself. I shit you not, the nigga's mouth is moving and he's moving his head around like it's multiple people in there talking to him. If I didn't need scapegoats, I'd kill all three of them. Killing my brother was a must. He was as much of a threat to my organization as Ice and Fame, so he had to go just like they do.

"Speak."

"Fame knows that Vince was turning on him. Ion think he ratted, but Fame is on high alert. Ice, on the other hand, that nigga don't know nothing. I got his bitch scared to even move without my command. If that don't work, I have a sure way we can get at them niggas."

"What's that?"

"Mama Rosemary. We kill that bitch, and it will criple them. She's the foundation them niggas stand on; without her, they're all lost."

"I like that plan. Figure it all out. Give these two something to do; I don't care what," I said dismissing them from my office.

"Oh boss trust, you're going to like what they got planned," he said with a smile as he led them out of my office.

I looked at the surveillance feed of my home. I have money in excess and more funneling in. Leaning back in my chair I started to reminisce on how it all started...

"Paulson! You got the newbie. Don't manage to fuck him up with all your bullshit. This is your last partner before I boot your ass down to traffic. Un fuck yourself!" the sergeant shouted. I hoped up rushing over to Officer Paulson, dropping my notepad and coffee in the process.

"Fuck!" I mumbled, rubbing the steaming hot liquid.

"Bull fucking shit, he stuck me with another throwaway," my partner said as all the other detective joined him in laughter. After cleaning up the spill, I rushed over to join him.

"Hi, I'm Stringer," I said, extending my hand to him. He looked at my hand he just stared at me looking like a fucking lame with my hand extended. Pulling my hand back, I looked at him expectantly.

"Meet me at the car in five," he said, walking off with the other officers.

I took a deep breath swallowing my nerves. It's my first day since graduating the academy, and I'm ready to start making a difference in the community. Things are fucked up out there, and I just want to show the kids that there's a way out. If I made it, then so can any other young man out there.

Making out to the parking zone, I searched for our squad car. I spotted an old banged up squad car that looked like it had to be operated by foot like the car from The Flintstones. Just my luck it was our car.

"What you too good for vintage, newbie?" Paulson asked, slipping his shades onto his eyes and taking a sip from his spiked coffee. It was more liquor than coffee, and he reeked of alcohol and cigarettes.

"No problem at all."

"Then get your ass inside."

Shaking my head, I hopped in the car. I see he was starting with the newbie hazing right away. Once inside the squad car, I pulled out my manual and note-book. He got in and stared from me to my notebook before laughing aloud. He laughed so hard and long that he nearly choked on the phlegm in his throat. I sat in my seat looking at him like he was fucking insane. Once he settled, he snatched my notepad and manual from hand tossing it out the window.

"Rule number one ass hat, none of that shit in that manual applies on the streets. We don't need the law because we are the law. Our way is what matters; fuck the regulations" he schooled me as he took off. Grabbing the log, I called off the first address, and he looked at me again before snatching it out of my hands and tossing it in the backseat.

"Rule number two. Fuck the log," he said in a cynical voice. Throwing my hands up towards the ceiling, I slid back in my seat relaxing. "You're a quick learner newbie makes me almost feel bad we won't be partners for long."

"What the fuck is that supposed to mean?"

"You'll see."

I sat up in the seat and watched him like a hawk. I might look like a square, but I'm a hood nigga, South Dallas born and raised. He gone have to bust a move. I watched him like a hawk as he continued to drive. He pulled up outside of a building that I knew all too well, and everything started to click.

"You're dirty?" I asked not really all to shocked.

"I got three kids, two ex-wives, and the force don't pay worth shit. You know how much it costs to support three households? Your new to this gig, kid. I was just like you once, but this job will rip your heart right out. You sacrifice everything for the shield only for the brass to swoop down and hold you up as the sacrificial lamb in a time of crisis," he said before taking a swig from his flask. He started coughing hard, and his skin turned bright pink. Shaking my head, I got out of the car and headed inside of my father's bar.

I walked inside, and it was packed with football fans. They were all huddled around the TV washing the Giants vs. The Bills play in the Super Bowl game. I stood for a few minutes catching a bit of it. I got money on the Giants this game. I got faith in my bet. One of my father's men walked over, taping me on the shoulder.

"The boss is waiting."

I looked at him before cutting my eyes back to the screen just as Norwood missed the field goal with a wide right kick, putting a load of money in my fucking pocket. Satisfied, I turned away and followed him to the back. We walked into the back room and down to the basement where my father ran his whore house. "Love Me Down" by Freddie Jackson was playing softly as I walked through the large open area. Men were seated in booths with women dancing, some topless, some completely naked. A few were having sex openly oblivious to our presence.

A beautiful brown skin woman caught my eye as she swayed in the middle of the floor. She got her hair done up in a short cut like Halle Berry. She had long slender legs with thick thighs and a round ass. Her small breasts were sitting up with her nipples poking straight out. I gave her another glance before making my way over to my father. He was up on the stage sitting on a throne with women flocking around him like he was a king. My disdain rose higher with every step I took.

"There's the heir to the throne," he boasted with a huge smile on his face.

"I don't want any parts of this shit."

With a quick snap of his fingers, everyone on the stage scattered starting a chain reaction. The music came to an abrupt halt; waitresses, hoes, and the johns all left in a huge stampede, leaving only my father, me, and his two bodyguards.

"I see that you got shit a little twisted. Everything that comes from me is mine, and my property moves in the way I see fit. I let you go off and join the academy, not because it's what you wanted, but because it's suited the needs of my operations. That pretty little bitch you got at home, I sent her your way. I picked your mother up for the gutter and made her mine so that she could bare me sons to inherit my operations.

I didn't do all this shit for you to look down your nose at me. You ain't shit but who the fuck I say you can be. You have no decision, and no fucking say so. Don't get shit twisted; I won't hesitate to kill you. Son or not no one goes against me. Now bow before your God," he said, and I kneeled before him.

"Now, since we got that shit clear. I'll let you go out and play good cop for a while. Let you see just how they'll treat you and you'll be running back. You have a month before I come and get you myself. Get the fuck out of my presence!"

Rising, I locked eyes with him. I'll let him think he's winning, but I'll die before I take part in any of this shit. Turning on my heels, I walked through the empty space and back up the stairs to the bar. Rushing out, I hopped in the car with my partner who was snoring like a bear.

"Paulson, let's fucking go!" I barked, causing him to jump up. After getting his head together, we headed out to actually do our fucking jobs.

~

Three days later

"Nunez and Sanders!" Sarge's loud voice carried out through the bullpen.

"They're out on a call," someone answered back

"Dixon and Frost!"

"In court," another person replied.

"Lomax and Reddi?"

"Just missed them."

"Is there anyone besides fuckup and junior fuckup that can take a call?" he asked sounding stressed.

I didn't say anything or take it personally because it was a dagger to Paulson more than me. I'm the newbie; he has ten years on the force and still gets zero respect. I continued to fill out the paperwork as if he hadn't said a word.

"They're the only ones in, Sarge," the desk clerk replied, and he sighed heavily.

"Paulson and Stringer your up. I gotta a complaint about a disturbance in the condos downtown," he said, handing me the papers.

"Paulson, don't pull any of your shit. Get the statement and leave," he said before we headed off without so much as a word to one another.

We drove to the building in silence. I had no words for him, and he had none for me. Neither of us gave a damn either way. Pulling up to the upscale building, he put the car and park giving me a look.

"I guess you're going to learn the lesson quicker than I suspected."

I got out of the car ignoring his comment. My mind was wondering to all the ways I had my wife pussy spread all over our home last night. I could care less what the fuck Paulson had to say. He gives the uniform a bad name anyways. Stepping off the elevator, we walked up to the door, and I knocked. A female flung the door open in a panic. She fell into my arms hysterically crying. Her face was badly beaten and coated with her blood.

"Ma'am who did this?" I asked trying to calm her, but she was far too distraught. Looking up at Paulson, he seemed unfazed by it all. The motherfucker was just leaned up against the wall looking off.

"Ma'am, I need you to calm down and tell me what happened. Is your attacker still inside?" She nodded her head, yes, and I hopped up rushing inside, clearing the rooms according to protocol. Upon entering the bedroom, I saw a man lying in bed smoking a cigarette. His hands were stained with the woman's blood. That was all I need for an arrest.

"Get up from the bed and drop to your knees. NOW!" I barked, and he just looked at me and chuckled.

"You must not know who I am."

"Get on the fucking ground and put your hands behind your head now!" I repeated, stepping closer to him with my gun aimed at his chest.

"You're toast," he replied, standing up from the bed and doing as told. I read him his rights and walked him out of the house and into the hall.

"It was nice knowing you, newbie," Paulson said still in the same spot as I left him. I ignored him and carried the suspect down to the car.

The ride back to the station was a quiet one. I was happy as hell to have my first collar, which was going to be a slam dunk case. Arriving at the station, I escorted the suspect inside to have him booked, but the Sarge met us at the doors.

"Release him!" he ordered, causing me to look at him oddly.

"He's a suspect."

"No, you fucking idiot. He's the mayor's son, and you just lost all fucking chances of ever receiving a promotion. Uncuff him and meet me in my office. Next fucking time you take a call from the city's elite you take fucking notes and leave. Are you a fucking retard! You don't fucking arrest the mayor's son!" he shouted.

I felt myself grow tense as I uncuffed him. How the fuck does this mother-fucker get off. I angrily walked to the Sarge's office in a bad fucking mood. I stormed in slamming the door.

"He fucking beat her!" I shouted, catching the Sarge by surprise.

"No shit! He beats her every Thursday night then Friday morning her takes her to Tiffany's, and she forgets all about it. Now sit your ass down, newbie!" he ordered. Biting back my response, I sat in the seat.

"You're fucking suspended for three months and you better pray it isn't made permanent once the mayor gets wind of this shit. I don't know what the fuck they were serving to you newbies in the academ.. You don't fucking arrest the city's elite under any circumstances. Their money built this fucking force you dipshit. Leave your badge and gun and get out of my office. You can kiss ever making detective goodbye. You just earned yourself a permanent spot on the beat with the resident fuckup, Paulson. I guess you two were a match made in heaven after all." Throwing my gun and badge down, I walked out of his office fuming.

"I warned you, kid," Paulson said as I stepped outside of the building, and I punched him in the jaw. My fist connected with a loud crunch and he laid on the ground groaning in pain.

"Stay the fuck out of my face with that shit!" I snapped, walking towards my car.

I drove around for hours before I found myself going to my father's bar. He was fucking right. The system I held so high shitted on me for doing what I vowed to do. If they can be above fucking justice, then so can I. Walking down into the brothel I notice the same woman with the Halle Berry cut. She was walking around serving drinks. I caught her eyeing me, and I licked my lips at her as I made my way back to my father's office. He was sitting behind his desk puffing on a cigar.

"I knew you'd come. I heard about the incident that happened earlier today. What took you so long, son?"

"I had to clear my head. So what does all of this intel? I just sit behind the desk and snap my fingers." He chuckled at my comment, taking a pull on his cigar and blowing a thick cloud of smoke in the air.

"All of that will come, but first I need an insurance policy."

"What you mean by that?"

"Go with Joe and Max."

Reluctantly, I followed them up the stairs and out of the building to their Lincoln, climbing in the back. It was dark out I was in the back getting irritated as they scanned the road. Max tapped Joe, and I followed their gaze to a Hispanic girl walking down the sidewalk. She had a bag in her hand like she was coming from a store. They slowly followed her until she cut through a park. Parking the car, they got out with me curiously following.

"Go rape that girl," Joe said, causing me to look at him with wide eyes.

"Hell no! What the fuck is wrong with you?" Max pulled his gun and cocked it back.

"Either you rape that bitch, or you die. Those are the fucking rules," Joe explained. Looking back and forth between the two, I knew they were serious.

Shaking my head, I took off in a light jog silently telling myself just to run the fuck away and forget about all of this shit. I slowed to walking pace when I got closer to her. Looking back, I noticed that Joe and Max were right on my heels. There was no escaping. Swallowing my nerves, I grabbed her up by her hair slammed her to the ground as she kicked and screamed.

Oddly, the protest was slightly arousing as I ripped her panties off from underneath her dress. Undoing my fly, I entered her and roughly fucked her tight pussy. She was so tight that I knew she had to be a virgin. Guilt turned into arousal as I raped her roughly. I felt her began to struggle less, and I knew it was because her body was accepting me. She clenched me with her walls, and I came inside of her. I paused on top of her for a minute to gain my breath, but she started to fight again, so I punched her in the head knocking her out. Easing out of her, I fixed myself and walked away from her unconscious body feeling my guilt rise.

"It's cool. We all felt guilty with our first one, but soon you'll start to crave it when they fight like that. That one had a lot of fight in her too," Joe said with Max agreeing.

I just ignored them both and walked along with my head cast down. I just raped an innocent fucking girl. The whole ride I was zoned out just thinking about what the fuck I did. I was so caught up in the moment of how good it felt that I drowned her cries out taking over her innocent body. When we got back to the bar, I stayed upstairs sitting at the bar tossing back shots.

"What's got you so stressed?" Halle Berry cut said.

"I've had a long day." She reached her hands down, grabbing and a handful of my dick.

"Well, let me help you with that. I'm Denise, but everybody calls me Nisey," she whispered into my ear, giving me a soft wet kiss.

"You can just call me daddy," I said, standing on my feet walking downstairs with her. Pushing her into the first booth I could find, I slid right into her mixing her juices with the girl I had just raped. Spreading her legs wide and pinning them to the side of her shoulders, I fucked her long and hard.

"YES! Fuck me, daddy, oh shit!" I bit down on my lips thrusting harder as her walls sucked me in deeper. Squeezing her thighs harder, I took out my frustrations on her pussy giving her vicious strokes that made her wetter and wetter. My dick was swimming in her ocean.

"You like this dick, don't you?" I grunted, slapping her in the face.

"I fucking love this big dick. Fuck me harder!"

Grabbing her by the neck, I slammed into her over and over fucking her so hard that it looked like she was having a seizure. I fucked her at that pace until we both came, and I collapsed beside her.

"Since, I'm going to be running this shit now. You are not to fuck any other man but me," I spoke seriously. She has some pussy that'll make me leave my wife for her. Ion know where this shit is going, but she'll be there with me every step of the way. Her pussy is too good to pass up.

FIFTEEN

Trouble

"Ok, bro so what was going on with you and Lai?" Ice asked as we headed back to Mama Rosemary's.

"The bitch is sneaking around, and she's got Mama lying for her ass. She keeps saying she's heading to Mama's house, but I know that shit a lie. She never takes one of the cars, and I got a tracker on Mama's BMW, so I know she ain't been picking her ass up. So how the fuck has she been getting there? She got me focused on all the wrong shit right now. I'm so busy worrying about this shit and watching her that I can't even focus on finding the nigga that shot her stupid ass."

"That's some of that Shanty shit. Yo, maybe one of those niggas from the wedding has been hitting her up. Females love hooking they friend up and shit," Fame said, making me get tight.

"How is she getting anywhere when her ass ain't got a fucking cellphone?"

"Nigga, they could be sending Morse codes and shit. Check the roof of your building for carrier pigeons. These broads are crafty. I saw a video of a bitch cloning her nigga's phone. Bro, she bought a new iPhone and had all his shit coming straight to that hoe." The fuck was this nigga talking about.

"Man, when Shanty left yo ass she took the last of your brain too, didn't it?" Ice asked, and they got started going back and forth.

"Fuck you, nigga. Niyah sucked yo balls up her loose ass pussy. Got you out here living like Caitlyn Jenner. Nigga, you're a fucking man bitch. Get the fuck outta here with that shit."

That shit had me weak I almost wrecked laughing at that nigga. Ice knows not to fuck with Fame on that joking shit. That nigga comes out with off the way shit that you can't even come back at.

"At least I got a bitch. Fuck you, ole lonely ass nigga," Ice retorted, sounding salty as hell.

"Nigga, it's still all love, Ice-Ice baby," Fame said, smiling.

"Yea, whatever bro."

"Nigga, you're saltier than the sweat between a fat bitch's titties. Loosen up," Fame said, leaning up between the seats.

This nigga act like a little kid sometimes. We joked some more until we pulled up to the house. We all hopped out and headed inside. I must've thought shit was sweet cause mama was on my ass with that back scratcher as soon as I hit the door. I guess it wasn't doing the job cause she dropped it and squared up on my ass, straight jawing my ass back to back. I ate that shit and let her get it out.

"I told you about that crazy shit, didn't I? You and Tyrell think it's ok to hit on women." She was landing every lick. She had a rhythm going about the shit. She got in one lick every two words. My face, neck, arms, and back were on fire.

"Y'all got me fucked up. Lai, pick that back scratcher up and beat his ass; and I want you to raise a hand to her in my face," Mama threatened.

Lai eagerly picked the back stretcher up and started going in. Her licks were harder than Mama Rosemary's. She had some animosity behind her shit. Feeling my anger rise, I reached out and bear hugged her close, yanking the back scratcher from her hand tossing it to Fame. He knew to get rid of that shit.

"Get y'all asses out my house now! I love you dearly but I done had enough damn stress! Goodbye," Mama said, walking off and heading up stairs.

I damn near drug Lai from the house. She got shit fucked up if she thinks I'm going for this bullshit. Sneaking around, lying, and laying hands on me; ian for that crazy shit. She's about to get a refresher course on who the fuck she's fucking with. Parking outside, I hopped out, ordering her to fucking follow. As soon as we got inside, I drug her ass down the stairs. Pushing her to the ground, I grabbed the chain to lock her ass back up. She acted like she had more sense then, and I could trust her to do what the fuck she was told without trying to sneak around.

"What are you doing with that?" she asked, scooting back on her ass.

I gave her a look, and she froze in place. She knows I'm not playing this bullshit with her. She gone act like a bitch with some sense, or she's going back to house bitch status. She got me fucked up. All that mushy shit wore off when she started trying to fucking play me. Ian falling for none of that shit. I reached my hand out for her ankle, and she quickly scurried away.

"Please don't do this. I'm sorry!" She had tears rolling down her face, but I didn't feel an ounce pity for her ass. Snatching her ankle, I snapped the cuff on. "Please!" She tried to grab my arm, but I stood to my feet pushing her off me.

"Go to the fucking corner."

"Don't do this to me, please. I'm sorry! Please" she sobbed, sniffing, and wiping snot with her hands "Baby, please! I love you, I'm sorry!"

"NOW!"

My voice blared so loudly that the room seemed to shake. It startled her, causing her to rush over to the corner furthest from the bed. I don't fucking want to hear that crying shit. She should be lucky I'm chaining her up and not beating her. My fucking body is sore, and I know I got bruises.

After a hot shower, I tried to lie down, but Lai was still in the corner crying. Not in the mood to be near her or hear her, I headed upstairs. I need to do the shit I was supposed to do instead of constantly keeping tabs on her. I went through my email searching for the video Syrina sent me. She was able to get video from the day Lai was shot.

I watched it three or four times slowing it down more and more before I was able to catch the nigga's reflection off the door of a car. Blowing and cleaning the image up best I could, I printed it out then headed back down to see if Lai know the nigga that shot her. From the stairs, I heard her down there singing negro spirituals like an old slave bitch.

Shaking my head, I headed further down the stairs slowly, approaching her. I knew that she felt me standing there, but she was refusing to look at me. She stopped singing and started humming as she rocked back and forth with a new wave of tears forming. She was starting to make me feel bad with the way she was acting.

"Do you know who this is?" I held the picture up so that she could see it. She stared at it for a minute then started back crying, making me want to slap her ass.

"Do you know the nigga?"

"It's my ex-boyfriend, James. I haven't seen him in years. Why do you have his picture?"

"Why would he want to shoot you?"

"I don't know."

"You been sneaking around to fuck this nigga?" I asked, snatching her to her feet ready to knock the fuck out of her.

"NO!"

I shoved her down, rushing upstairs. I grabbed my bottle and sat at the dining room table taking it to the fucking head. I sat back in the chair wondering how much I'd miss her if I just killed her ass. The shit would save me a lot of fucking stress. She got my nerves all fucked up with this crazy shit. I sat drinking my anger away and out of nowhere, I heard buzzing. *I'm fucked up.* I stared at the bottle for a minute before pushing it aside. The shit got me hearing noises. Throwing my head back on the chair, I rubbed my face and sighed heavily, getting my mind right before I go down there with Lai.

BUZZZZZZ! BUZZZ! BUZZZZZZ!

Standing up from the chair, I followed the sound. It was coming from the wall. Placing my hand flat against it, I felt around to find the source of the vibration. Tapping against the bricks, I noticed one was lose. Pulling it out, I found an iPhone tucked in the back. Clutching it tightly in my fist, I punched the fucking wall with my left hand, bloodying my knuckles. My hand stung and started to swell, but I couldn't focus on that because I wanted to fucking murder that bitch. My anger took over, and I took off towards the stairs. The phone started buzzing, stopping me in my tracks. Looking down, it was texts and missed calls on the screen. That nigga was begging Lai to go away with him to help him kick his drug habit.

I unlocked the phone, and I scrolled through the messages eating all that shit. At first, I thought the bitch was sneaking, but now I see that she's just fucking stupid. This nigga was sleepwalking her ass into a fucking trap, and I can see that shit. Turning in the opposite direction, I headed up the stairs to my office. I sat at my desk pulling up the security video from the cameras I placed inside of Lai's crib. The video confirmed everything I knew. I got up and headed downstairs. I gotta explain shit to her simple-minded ass like I'm talking to a fucking toddler because she can't grasp simple shit.

"What happened to your hand?" Pulling the keys from my pocket with my good hand, I tossed them to her and sat on the bed.

"Go get the first aid kit," I said not even bothering to look at her. She rushed over and brought back the shit for me to clean up my hand. She tried to clean it, but I snatched away.

"Why are you being like this!" Snatching the phone from my pocket, I threw it at her, hitting her in the face.

"Thought you wasn't being sneaky."

"I'm not." Just that quick, I had her by her throat with my good hand. This bitch thinks I'm fucking stupid.

"Ok! Ok!" she whispered weakly.

I wasn't letting go. I'm sick of this relationship shit already so maybe I should just choke her to fucking death. She got me mad and fucking my hand up over bullshit. Seeing that I had no intention of letting her ass go, she reached over and hit my wounded hand making me let her go. She fell to the floor crying and gasping for air.

This is the shit that I fucking hate. I should never have gone back. When I let her go I should've just stayed the fuck away. I gotta handle them niggas that's plotting on her so that I can just let her go about her way cause if not, I'm going to kill her. Blood from my swollen hand dripped to the floor as I stood over her staring a hole into her face.

"I can't keep doing this shit with you. This shit ain't for me. Stay your ass here until I get back. That nigga you been texting is plotting up against you with that nigga that shot you. They were going to lure your ass out somewhere and torture you. Don't fucking leave!" I sat back on the bed and wrapped my hand up before getting dressed in all black and grabbing my hunting knife and my guns.

"What are you going to do?" she asked with fearful eyes.

"Everything in my fucking power to protect you. Stop trusting every fucking body from your past. You started over leaving them behind for a fucking reason; stop being so fucking dumb. Stay here!"

I walked up the stairs and out the front door, hopping into my ride heading to lay these fuck niggas down. They're crazy as hell to think they could lure her into a trap without me finding out.

SIXTEEN

James

"Keep texting her! We have to get this done tonight. Make her come," I urged Jacob as I paced back and forth.

"What the hell do you think I'm doing? Sit the hell down. You're making me dizzy."

"You aren't doing enough! We NEED her here tonight," I shouted!

"No, YOU NEED to calm down. Are you off your meds or something?"

Lie, you can't trust him.

"No! I take them every day. I'm just ready to get this shit over with. Do you think she knows about our plan?"

"No she doesn't," he said, looking around nervously. I stopped moving and stared at him. *He's against you. You can't trust him.*

"You're setting me up."

"Dude, what the fuck are you talking about right now? Why would I set you up? Malaika fucked my life up just as bad as she did yours. My sister's death ruined my family, and I'm a fucking coke addict because of her. Get your head on straight, or this shit will fall apart. I'm going to text her one last time saying that I'm having suicidal thoughts."

It's a trick.

"No, I think we can trust him."

"Trust who? Dude you're really starting to freak me out. The pacing, twitching, and mumbling is weird enough, but now you're speaking out loud to yourself. Where are your meds?" He got up from the couch trying to go near my duffle bag that was sitting by the door.

"NO!"

I pushed him back before he could get to it. If he goes through my bag, he'll see my notes. I never planned to kill Malaika. I just needed their help to get close to her so that I can take her home with me. I have a cabin for us in Oklahoma. It has everything we will need to start our family. I know that once I get her there, she'll love it and realize that she was just being silly. She didn't mean those things she said about me. She was just speaking from guilt.

"Dude, relax. I'm just trying to fucking help you!" he shouted, getting up from the ground.

He's going to try to sneak over there. He doesn't trust you. You have to kill him; he'll keep Malaika from you.

"You're right."

"Right about what? James, bro, we've always been cool, but you're blowing my high and freaking me out. I'm just going to leave. If Malaika's comes just have whoever is talking to you up there help you with her."

He tried running to the door, but I quickly raced behind him bashing his head into the wall knocking him out. I drugged his body into the bedroom and tied his hands and feet with bed sheets.

"*You have to kill him*," one voice said as I paced back and forth.

"*He'll keep her from you. He wants her all to himself*," another added. I stopped pacing, clutching my head trying to get a moment of silence, but the chatter wouldn't stop.

Kill him!

Kill him!

You know what you have to do.

You'll never have her.

They'll get to her before you do.

Maybe you don't deserve her.

KILL HIM!

KILL HIM!

DO IT! DO IT! DO IT!

Pulling the butcher's knife from my waistband, I rushed over plunging it into his body over and over, praying that my actions will quiet the voices, but it only fueled the rants. They turned it into a cheer of sorts as they continued to boom through my head.

KEEP GOING!

DON'T STOP!

MORE!

MORE!

MORE!

CUT OUT HIS HEART TO GIVE IT TO HER AS A GIFT!

YEA! DO IT!

DO IT! DO IT!

Obeying their wishes, I used my foot to crush his rib cage, then I took the knife and carved out his heart. I held I up in the air with a wide grin. It was beautiful. Malaika's going to love it. As I held it in the air admiring it, the door burst open.

"What the fuck? Nigga, you on that Norman Bates shit?" Trouble shouted.

Before I could react my body was riddled with bullets. All that could be heard was the air whistle as the bullets exited the silencer. I fell to the ground still clutching the heart.

"Give her my gift!" I struggled to say as I tried to hold up the heart for him to take. He gave me an odd look as he stood directly over my body.

"This will be the best gift she'll ever get," he said before aiming the gun at my head and pulling the trigger. Still, I have no regrets because I died loving Malaika. One day we will be reunited, and she will be mine for eternity.

SEVENTEEN

Shanty

"Love, did you look at that information I sent you today?' Neron asked as he stood in front of our bed, slipping out of all his clothes. Fame's sleeping in only underwear had rubbed on me, and I transferred it to Neron.

I hadn't heard anything he said because I was staring hard at his print. His dick was sitting against his thigh playing peek-a-boo with me from the bottom of his boxers on the left side. I just wanted to go over and lick it so damn bad.

"Did you hear me, love?"

"Huh?" He gave me a slight chuckle and head shake before fixing himself.

"Did you look at the material I sent?"

"Um yes, I did," I replied, sitting against the headboard. He's in business mode now, and there is no hope of me getting dicked down until we have this discussion. His ass is so serious sometimes.

"Did you understand all of it?"

He slid into the bed next to me grabbing his iPad Pro, tapping at something on the screen, while I was sitting there trying to figure out a way to tell him that I don't care about the various energy sources nor how they affect technology and all that shit. That's his forte, not mine, but being the supportive wife I am, I'll be a team player.

"All of it except hydroelectricity and wind turbines. That shit really had me lost."

He took the time to explain it all to me, and I caught on. I think it's kind of cool that movement can be turned into an electrical current.

"Ok babe, I understand all of that now, but why are you pressing so hard for me to learn? This is like the twelfth thing you've sent me this week. I feel like I'm in college all over again. You got my damn brain hurting." I added a little pout hoping it would make him feel bad enough to stop sending me shit. I love what he does but can a bitch love it in theory? I don't want to know the ins and outs. I liked having the general idea.

"There may come a time where I may not be able to fulfill my duties, and I need to know that you know enough to act in my best interest."

"What you mean? Is there something you need to be telling me?"

"Calm down, love," he said, grabbing my arm and pulling me towards him. He probably senses that I was ready to start swinging or something. He's talking like he knows something I don't know.

"I'm a businessman, so it's in my nature to plan for things that may never happen. I want to make sure that we discuss everything so that if the time should come you know how to act. I own a successful corporation, as my wife you have to be cognizant of all things that concern me because they concern you as well."

"What are these things that I need to be aware of?" I didn't even bother to handle the attitude in my voice. We just got married, and he's talking about something bad happening. Could we at least get through the honeymoon phase first? I dislike this side of him.

"Don't be that way, love. I know you don't want to have this conversation, but it's necessary," he spoke softly, pulling me close. His ass he knew what he was doing. I held in my moan as he kissed on the side of my neck, but I still tilted my head giving him better access.

"I don't want to be hooked up to a ventilator, I've signed a DNR."

Just like that, he ruined the moment. Remember that record scratching moment when Trouble called Lai a bitch to me. Well, this is part two times ten of that. This was glass shattering, cat screeching vibes. I hopped up from the bed and just stared at him trying to hold in the tears.

"Why would you sign something like that Neron?"

"If I code I want to go. I don't want them bringing me back, and I could never imagine being hooked up to tubes. Love, when it's my time I just want to go peacefully and at once. No extraordinary measures."

"No! People have woken up from that before, Neron. They bring people back when they code all the time. You can't just give up. You have to want to fight!" I just don't understand how he could think like this. Why would he not want to fight to stay alive to do everything to come back to me? He pulled me close and stared deeper into my eyes.

"The odds of those things happening aren't in my favor. I love you, but I need you to respect my wishes and understand that I do not want them to hook me up to those machines. I watched my mother hang on to my father for a year; hoping that he would come back, but he was long gone. They had tubes breathing for him, feeding him, and even cleaning his waste." He paused, giving himself time to reel in his emotions.

"Love, that can't be me. You have to let me go when it's my time, and you make sure my mother doesn't bully you into doing anything other than what I wish. She has clout, and she'll use it, but you'll have the ultimate say in everything. Don't let them turn me into a living corpse." A tear escaped his eye, and I climbed on top of him.

As much as it hurts to agree I have to respect what he wants, especially after seeing how emotional this makes him. That sad and bougie bitch can move the fuck around if she thinks she's gone be running shit. I fight old hoes too.

Shaking the thoughts, I looked into his eyes seeing he was still battling his emotions. I know just how to ease his mind though.

Climbing out of his lap, I got on my knees, pulling his big chocolate dick from his briefs. I flicked my tongue back and forth around the head, causing him to grow longer in my hands.

"Fuck!" he groaned, palming my head and pushing my mouth onto him. I took him in with my jaw tight bobbing like a buoy in the middle of the ocean.

"SSSSSSS!" he hissed as I took as much of his long fat dick down my throat.

I stuck my tongue out allowing a little more to slip in, and he gripped my hair tighter grinding in circles in my throat. The movements made my pussy tingle, and it felt like he was grinding all up in it instead of my mouth. Giving Neron head have me coming like we were fucking because he gets so into it.

"Gag on that shit." He said in a deep growl. I looked up at him, and he was biting down on his bottom lip completely taken over by lust. I started gagging letting the wetness seep from my lips as I gave him sloppy head.

"I'm about to cum love!" he grunted, gripping my hair.

I sucked him in as far as he could fit and tightened my cheeks around him, milking him for all his sweet potion. His sperm was enchanted; it makes a bitch leak like the waterfalls in fairytales. He came long and hard down my throat, and I swallowed it all.

"Bring that ass here!" he demanded, lifting me up and tossing me onto the bed. He grabbed my underwear ripping them off, but the bedside phone beeped signaling that someone was calling from the guard's house out front.

"Ignore it," I whined, wanting my head. He obeyed and yanked my panties off diving into my pussy head first. In the first ten second, I was headed up for the stars as his tongue was set on Bust Rhymes flow.

"Sir, you have a guest by the name of Malaika Coleman here. She says it's an urgent matter." Trevor's voice echoed through the speaker system. Hopping up, I reached over hitting the button beside the bed.

"Let her through." Neron got up, but I pulled his ass right back down. That urgent matter ain't stopping me from getting my nut.

I swear I really didn't mean to fall asleep without checking on Lai, but the way Neron's pipe game is set up, I be too fucking worn out and tired to do any fucking thing but catch them Zs. She must be ok because she never came to the room searching for me. Feeling slightly guilty, I got my ass out of bed and handled my hygiene quickly before going to see about her. Neron was lightly snoring when I left our bedroom. I walked down the halls searching all the guest room until I finally found the room Lai was asleep in. Of course, she'd pick the smallest room in the whole house.

"Lai!" I called out lightly tapping on the door and pushing it open.

I could hear her humming, and she was rocking herself, so I knew she was upset. I walked over to the bed and climbed in with her. She turned to face me, and her face was soaking wet from her tears. Her eyes were bloodshot red, but the minute they locked with mine, she became hysterical.

"I-I-I-I thought I could change him, Shanty! I thought my love could make him love me back, but he doesn't. He locked me back up and walked away tossing me aside like I was trash. This is not love," she cried as pulled her to my chest and cradled her.

"Does he know you're here?"

"No, I left while he was out. He's probably still gone."

I didn't mean to not address her issues, but if he knows she came here, we have to leave because Trouble is coming for her. With the way Neron has our security set up, it won't be nothing nice when he gets here. Lai and I need to go to the one place that I know he will not dare come to act crazy.

"Come on, let's go to Mama Rosemary's." Reluctantly she got up and headed down to my car while I told Neron what happened and where I would be. When I got to the car, she was just sitting there staring out into space.

"I know that it hurts right now, but you're doing what's best for you. You have to show him that the way he treats you isn't right. Put yourself first, and he will follow if he truly cares about you." She looked over at me and just stared for a while.

"I don't know how. How can I put myself first when all I want is for him to want me? I did everything for him to love me and he doesn't," she cried, and I pulled her into another hug. She had me crying my eyes out right along with her. When we finally made it to mama's house, it was nearing six in the morning. She had a strange car in her yard, but ian have time to discuss that cause I was too fucking tired. She can explain to me why she's fucking Big Dee when I wake up. She had better hope he's gone before the three stooges pop up cause shit is gone get too real in this house. I almost want to tell them myself because she is just wrong for robbing the damn cradle like that.

EIGHTEEN

Fame

My doorbell rang causing me to pop up out of my sleep. Climbing out of bed, I headed down snatching the door open. Shanty was standing there in in a tan trench coat with some red heels on and bright red lipstick. Her hair was pulled up into a sexy messy bun with pieces hanging down. I just stared and her because she was so fucking beautiful and sexy.

"What are you doing here?" I asked, licking my lips.

Instead of answering, she pushed me aside and strutted through my foyer and into the family room. She pulled the belt of her coat undoing the knot, letting it slip down her body. She was ass naked underneath, and her body was perfect. My dick was reaching for my knees looking at her. I was stuck like a muh'fucka just standing there staring at her sexy ass body.

"I know you've been sitting outside my job every day watching me. So, I thought I'd come and give you something great to watch," she said playfully biting her nail as she looked over her shoulder sashaying to the couch. She sat down and spread her legs wide for me.

"I know you love it when I play in, daddy. If you make that nut shoot far enough, I'll let you taste it," she taunted in a seductive purr. I freed my dick from my pajamas and started stroking my shit as she rubbed her fingers in her wet pussy. She took two fingers and turned them to me showing me how wet that pussy was. I was so fucking turned on that my dick started aching.

"Make that shit talk for me, Shanty." She took her fingers and pushed them deep inside of her going fast, and that pussy was speaking in tongues. You could hear the smacking noises echoing off the walls. I beat my dick faster to match her pace, and it felt like her pussy was gliding up and down my shaft as I watched her beating that pussy up with her fingers.

"Pinch them nipples!"

"Aah!" She moaned at the sensation, and that shit sent chills up my spine. I wanted to be inside her so fucking bad, but I gotta buss first.

"Get loud and nasty for daddy."

She took her finger from her pussy and stuck them in her mouth sucking them clean before pulling them out and letting saliva drip onto them. She then rubbed her wet fingers all over her pussy, smearing it with her juices. Taking two fingers, she placed them deep and inside fucking herself as she moaned and screamed out. She squirted out, and the sight sent my nut shooting out like I was popping champagne.

"Come taste it, daddy." She didn't have to tell me twice. I rushed over, but a hard smack hit me across the face.

"Wake the fuck up, old pervert ass nigga!"

I hopped up sitting straight up in the bed. Trouble and Ice were standing next to my bed laughing like shit was funny.

"Shanty, oh Shanty. Nigga, you were in yo sleep moaning like a bitch," Ice mocked.

"Nigga, fuck you! Why the fuck y'all come in here fucking with me? That's some bitch ass shit. I was just about to taste the pussy and you nigga come in fucking shit up. I be having a hard time dreaming about Shanty."

"Bro shut the fuck up with that freak nasty shit and go shower. Lai left my ass and ran to Mama house. Ian trying to go over there by myself cause I know she got the back scratcher waiting," Trouble said looking scared.

"The fuck me being there gone do?"

"You always fucking up, so I know she got a reason to get yo ass."

"I'ight, get the fuck out so I can shower then, nigga."

"Nigga, we already know you had a high school moment on your covers," Ice joked as they left out the door.

I wanted to get up and knock his ass out, but I got a big ass nut stain on the front of my drawers. Them nigga would have clowned the fuck out of my ass. Once they left, I hopped out of bed and hit the showers. I can still jack my dick to the pieces of the dream I remember. I'm still at them niggas head for fucking my moment up though.

"Yo ain't that Big Dee's whip?" Ice said as we pulled up Mama's street.

"Hell yea, that's the nigga's ride. The fuck he doing over here this early?"

"Ion know, but we bout to see," Trouble said, throwing his truck in park.

We all hopped out at the same time, and I rushed through the door. The nigga wasn't in the family room, den, nor the kitchen. My pride wouldn't let me fucking believe he was upstairs with my mama. That nigga ain't that fucking stupid. I continued to search the base level of the house. I even went into the fucking basement. Pissed, I started yelling.

"MAMA!" Trouble and Ice were on the same shit.

All of us were scared to go up the stairs into that room. I can't see no nigga lying in bed with my mama. I need that nigga to get dressed and come down here to face his fate. I damn near would rather he cross me on the business tip than to fuck my mama.

"MAMA!" the three of us said in unison this time. Shanty and

Lai came rushing down, and I almost got caught up staring at her thick ass in her pajamas set, but I didn't trip on it.

"Why the hell are y'all in my house hooping and hollering like wild hogs?"

She was walking down in one of those silk lingerie robes letting me know she fuck that nigga, and I lost it. I ran up the stairs pushing past her and heading straight for her room. This nigga was sitting on her bed putting on his shoes.

"My fucking mama!" I barked, running up.

I knocked that nigga across his shit, hard as fuck. The nigga ate that lick and popped me back. From there we were at it fucking mama's room up. Big Dee ain't no fucking joke cause this nigga had major pressure behind his blows, but my shit was quick as lightning with the force of a semi-truck. I wasn't letting up on his ass, until I felt the familiar pain of that fucking back scratcher. She started eating my ass up with that bitch as I stood there and took it. Big Dee thought the shit was sweet, but as soon as she got off my ass, she was on his.

"Y'all got me fucked up, fighting in my fucking house. Get the fuck downstairs and sit at my fucking kitchen table! Every damn body go NOW!" Her voice was loud enough to be heard in Egypt as she shouted. We all got our asses up and headed down the stairs piling around the kitchen table like a bunch of kids getting scolded.

"I bet you feel simple as hell getting handled just like us. You still a little ass kid in her mind, fuck nigga!"

"Fame, bro, it's always been love between us, but ian taking no disrespect."

"Then move something, nigga!" We both stood on our feet ready to jack again, but she came back, wrapping us around the back of our neck with the back scratchers. She had two out, one in each hand.

"One thing nobody gone do is disrespect my fucking house. If you want to be mad at somebody, be mad at me! But, you hold your ass on. I'm getting to you last," she said, extending her finger and turning away from me, focusing on Trouble. I sat there staring daggers at the nigga I called my right hand and my fucking bro! I made a gun with my hand aiming it at his forehead, letting that nigga know that his days were numbered.

"Whenever, wherever," he retorted.

Mama turned back to face us giving us a stare, but that shit wasn't moving me. I'm at this nigga's head, and Fame gets his target ASAP. Ain't no borrowed time fucking with me.

"Donavan, get the fuck out my house and don't come back until you got some gah damn sense. Don't bring your ass around here fucking with Malaika. She's staying with me, and that's all you need to know now, go!"

I swear that nigga stared at mama like he wanted to murk her ass and she might never admit it, but she was probably shook. He nodded his head before looking at Malaika for a minute and walking out the door.

"Ignacio, go home and tend to that damn girl. That's right she called me on your ass now get the hell out and go work that shit out." Ice chuckled as he kissed her cheek and left out the house. That nigga is probably going to get up with Trouble. He's not fucking with Niyah like that right now.

"Shanty and Lai give us some privacy."

They hurried up and hauled ass out of there like they just had something they needed to talk about. They probably gone laugh at how mama whooped Big Dee and me with that heavy ass back scratcher. She grabbed an empty chair, pulling it close to Big Dee, grabbing the nigga's hand. He leaned in kissing her cheek, and the way she smiled pissed me off, so I hopped up.

"You're really fucking doing this? You're sitting up here with a nigga that's my fucking age?" The nigga looked like he was getting tight with what I said, and my trigger finger started burning. I wanted to shoot his ass so bad.

"You got a fucking problem speak dirty on it, nigga." I barked.

"You acting like a bitch right now."

"Let me roll up to your mom's crib, and then we can talk about bitches."

"Fuck you trying to say."

He stood up and just that fast I was at his head. We were fucking shit up, and not even the back scratcher could stop us. So, she just stood back screaming and crying. We bumped until we got tired and the nigga started staring at me. Tired of fighting I backed away, making my mind up at that moment that as soon as he dots that door, he's dead.

"I'm sorry if I hurt you son, but it's my time to be happy. I've been lonely all these years, and I finally have somebody that adores me. I ain't apologizing for falling in love damn it!" she screamed out, causing me to chuckle.

If she thought that shit was gone move me, she thought wrong. I ain't for this shit they got going and I never will be. I don't give a fuck if she felt like Jesus' handcrafted that nigga for her, ian feeling it.

"You can have a few more hours of being in love, but as soon as he exits that door, it's a wrap. You'll be praying to forget the images of his brains splattered on the pavement. Trust is everything to me and both of y'all disloyal. Ian feeling this shit and I never will. Big Dee, call your moms to start making the preparations. It's gone be a close casket, my nigga!" I spat, walking out of the kitchen.

Betrayed wasn't even the word for how I feel. When I came to her, Mama Rosemary promised me she'd never hurt me like my birth moms did, but it turns out that she's a hoe just like that bitch. She should have never fucked my homie, and he should have never crossed that line. They both fraud as fuck for the shit. Now it makes sense to why that nigga was suspect; he was sneaking behind my back to fuck my mama. This nigga is gone die slow and painfully.

"You good?" Trouble asked, rolling up on me as I walked down the street.

"Nah, let's sit right here and get comfortable. I'm killing that nigga as soon as he steps through that door."

"I'ight."

NINETEEN

Rosemary Little

Luther Vandross' "Always and Forever" played softly in the background of my dimly lit room. The candles flickered against the wall creating a more romantic effect. Devon was lying on my bed looking like the world sexiest teddy bear. At 6'4 over 250 pounds, he's a stocky caramel complexed sexy thang. On the outside, he appears mean and tough, but with me, he's as sweet as can be. In all my years, I never came home to a man doing something romantic for me.

"Go sit down so I can give you a foot massage."

Doing as I was told I sashayed my ass over to the chair and sat down handing him my foot. Soft and gently, he rubbed oil over my foot staring me deep in the eyes. He was massaging my foot so damn good that I felt my juices running. Hiking my dress up over my ass, I threw my head back as he slowly massaged me to the tip of an orgasm. I felt something warm wrap around my toes. I opened my eyes to him sucking on my big toe. I never had it before, but the way he was doing it caused me to scoot my ass down in the seat so that I could open my legs wider.

"You like that?"

"Yea, I like that shit," I moaned.

He slowly sucked each one of my toes causing my pussy to throb and pulsate. He slowly started licking his way up my legs until he got to my sugar bowl. Taking his long, thick tongue, he grazed the fabric of my lace panties. His tongue mixed with the fabric had a crazy sensation that I loved. Grabbing my legs, he yanked me so that my pussy was facing up. From there he spread my legs as far as they could go opening up my pussy exposing the inside within my black lace panties.

"I want to tease the pussy first," he said before diving in and licking my pussy through the fabric.

Something about that feeling was so fucking right. This young boy was teaching me thangs that I never knew I could like. He kissed and licked through the fabric until my panties were soaking wet. Slipping them off, he went right back to work taking big laps like he was drinking from a dog bowl before flicking his tongue faster than the speed of light. I gripped his head and shoved his face deeper. I wanted him to suck up all my sweet sugar water.

"Yea, eat this fucking pussy!"

Being a good boy, he went crazy on my ass and started sucking on my clit. I came hard in his mouth, causing him to slurp it all up and go right back to work. He had me clutching the seat of the chair for dear life as he made love to me with his thick tongue.

"You ready for the dick now?"

"Hell yea!"

"Put that fat ass in the air and let me see that pretty kitty kat."

Pulling my dress completely over my head and removing my bra, I switched over to the bed in my heels propping my ass in the air with chest flat on the bed. I had that old school arch that's about to make him lose his mind. These young hoes talk shit about us older women, but they could learn a thing or two from a seasoned woman such as myself. Walking over, he stopped admiring my ass before smacking it.

SMACK! SMACK!

"Keep that fat ass in the air!" he demanded as I wiggled it around. Popping me on the ass with his big dick a few times, he ran it up and down my wet pussy before plunging deep into my sugar bowl.

"SHHHHHH! This pussy is so fucking sweet on my dick! She got my shit coated!" As he plugged deep and deeper into me, I threw my ass back making sure to make my ass cheeks jiggle.

"Yea! Shake that fucking ass for me. Nut up on this shit, baby."

He gave me all the confidence I needed, and I took over throwing my ass back like a '98 Chevy, gripping him tighter and tighter with each thrust while he grabbed my waist squeezing me. I was trying to take his life from his body with my tight walls.

SMACK!

"FUCK."

SMACK!

"THIS."

SMACK!

"DICK."

"Shit, I'm about to cum!" I moaned still throwing it back. I felt him grow and twitch and I knew he was coming. He took over and fucked us both over our thresholds, and we fell our asses in the bed tired as hell. Fucking around with his good dick ass got me acting young. My damn back and hip is gone lock up on me by morning. I don't remember what time we fell asleep, but I remember waking up to Tyrell loud ass mouth, and I knew right then that shit was about to go bad. I threw on my robe and headed down to try to calm them down, but shit went all the way left.

~

Lord knows I never wanted my sons to find out about Devon like this, but I can't change what is done. I understand Tyrell's anger. That's why I chose to keep things from him. I knew that it would be ugly. Not that we are doing anything wrong because we are both fully grown, but this is the first time I've been this deep with a man. Don't be fooled. I was still getting dick, I just knew better than to bring it into my home. I had four children from unstable backgrounds they needed something stable. The man I was dealing with for years was everything but that. Chile, that negro thought his dick was meant to explore every pussy on earth. I deserved better than that and Devon gives me that love I need.

"Yo, I'm out." I stopped daydreaming and looked at him. I know he doesn't think he's about to leave.

"Just stay in here until I can talk some sense into him. Tyrell is upset right now, but when he calms down, I can work it out, baby. Just don't go out that door for him to kill you. Don't do that to me."

"Man, fuck all this shit. That nigga don't put fear in my heart. I move on my own accord!"

"So, fuck me then? When you take your ass out there and he kills you, fuck me?" Tears poured down my face as I spoke.

"Man, come here and stop that shit." He pulled me into his arms and kissed my forehead. "You know damn well I love you, and I don't want to do shit to hurt you, but I can't let that nigga think he pumps fear into my heart. Fame knows how I'm rocking, and we just gone have to shoot this shit out. I knew the risk when we started fucking around, but that shit still didn't stop us. I love you too much to walk away, so this how it's gone be."

"No, it's not. I'm about to go out there and talk to my children. I love you, and I love them, so nobody is shooting shit. Lay down and get ready for me when I get my ass back." I gave him a juicy kiss before heading outside to talk to my crazy ass children. They were parked outside my damn house, and I just knew they had a truck full of guns.

Shaking my head, I walked over, and Ignacio hopped out the from the truck, but I made him get back up there. I need to sit beside Tyrell right now to let him know I wasn't trying to hurt him by falling in love with Devon.

"You need to stop this foolishness, Tyrell."

"Trouble and Ice y'all hear something? Ion speak thot," he smarted, and I knocked fire from his ass.

"Donavan and Ignacio go in the house while I walk with Tyrell." They may not have wanted to, but they did what the hell I said.

"Get out and let's take a walk."

I met him around on his side, and we walked down the street

admiring all the beautiful houses. I've always been blessed to live in a great neighborhood. My husband died in the army during training when I was 21, and I just sunk into a bad place. Living in the great big house with no one to share it with became too much. I decided to take in foster children to fill the voids, and it did that and so much more. I love my children as if they were my own because to me they are mine.

"I wasn't trying to hurt you."

"But you did," he said roughly.

"I know that baby, and I'm sorry. Sorry for hurting you, but I'm not sorry for falling in love. I lost the love of my life, before we could really enjoy each other. I took in kids to get some of that love back, and you all gave me that and so much more, but y'all are grown. My life revolves around my grown kids, and I felt like I finally needed something for me. I'm sorry that he's your friend, but I love him. I haven't felt his nice since Grant died."

"I hear what you saying mama, but why did he have to be my nigga, though? You couldn't find somebody we don't know."

"Love chooses us, baby."

"Nah, ian trying to hear that shit. You could have come to me and told me straight up, but y'all were creeping around behind my back, that's the shit that fucks me up. You don't get many real niggas these days, and you just fucked our whole bond up by fucking my nigga. Ian never tried to get in the way or nothing you had going. I love you ma, and I want you to be happy. So, if Big Dee's doing it for you, rock with him, but ian here for it, period. Be happy and all that, but don't think that I'm accepting that nigga as my step daddy and all that other shit.

Ian rocking with you and him on no couple shit, so don't call me around when he's laying up with you. Don't try to include me in this fucked up family shit cause I'm gone spazz on it. I'll respect you if you respect my mental, without trying to force this relationship y'all got going on me cause I'm never gone like the shit. As far as I'm concerned the beef between me and that nigga is dead. Just let him know that ion fuck with him by any means. He can take over the shop in the south, but other than that ian got nothing for him."

I wanted so badly to make him understand, but I know that I can't. I guess the best thing about all of this is that he's not trying to kill Devon. That's the best I can ask for in this situation, so the rest I'm going to have to leave up to time. Time will tell us just how things play out. I finished talking to my baby boy, and before long he was back smiling and laughing. I know he's just hurt because he feels like we betrayed him, but I would never do nothing like that to my kids.

Like I said Devon was just who I needed to bring me back to life after all these years of carrying that torch for my dead husband. Even if things don't workout, I will still always love his young ass for knocking the dust and dirt off this old pussy. He took my shit from looking like an old haunted house to a spanking brand-new mansion. My sugar bowl has been good and juicy every day since we started messing around. Shit, Rosemary, got her groove the fuck back!

TWENTY

Lai

I sat up on the bed staring out into space. Shanty was busy texting Neron and giggling like a schoolgirl. Meanwhile, my mind is on a rampage. She comes over every day after work, and all she does is text on her phone. I like it better when Niyah comes because at least I can play with Anju while she complains about Ice not dealing with her. I have so much on my mind that I don't even know where to begin talking about everything.

The night I left, I took a pregnancy test that I bought on one of the days I snuck out. I'm carrying his child. I knew that something was off when I didn't have my period after two weeks. At first, I thought that it could have been from stress, but I remember that Trouble never pulls out. I'm excited and scared about everything. Actually, the baby is the major reason that I left. I can't imagine us being parents when he's constantly hitting me and locking me up.

He has a lot of work to do within himself before I can even consider going back and I've made that very clear through our messages. He texts and calls me constantly, so much that I regret buying a phone. Feeling too conflicted inside, I grabbed my guitar and just started singing. The first song that came to mind was "How Can I Ease The Pain" by Lisa Fischer.

Before I could even get into the second verse tears poured down my face. I just broke down and let it all out. Shanty turned over and pulled me into her arms hugging me tightly. This is what I needed her for more than anything, just to know that she's here and that she understands.

"That song is one that I used to have on repeat. She was calling to my soul when she sang that shit. You ease the pain by putting Malaika first. Stop thinking so much about him, and do what you have to do to make sure that you are happy with or without him. That will ease it all, trust me."

"Shanty, I don't think I've ever been truly happy. All I can ever remember is being alone and having everything I could ever want."

"Then you have to address that. You and Trouble live your lives avoiding the past. Go straighten all that shit out Lai, and then start doing what it takes for you to be happy. You're about to be a mother soon. I know you ain't trying to bring your child into the world with a unstable mother. I see too many cases of women having children when they aren't in a stable place mentally, emotionally, or physically. You have to be all the way together in order to handle things. Too many women suffer from postpartum and other things, Lai. Trouble threw you off from your counseling. Now, that he's not in the picture at the moment you need to start back focusing on your peace of mind."

"You're right. I think I'm going to finally take that trip to visit my parents. It times that we all sit down and settle things."

"True. Now sing something happy to change the mood before I leave. My husband's sitting butt naked in the bed waiting for me."

I laughed so that hard tears feel down. She's so damn nasty, but I'm happy for her words of encouragement. I really needed that to give me the boost to go visit my parents.

~

I pulled up to the home I grew up in, and nothing seemed to change. The driveway looked the same down to the huge fountain with an angel in the center. I can bet they still have my name etched in the bottom. I parked Mama Rosemary's car and got out slowly. Gaining the courage, I walked up to the door and heading inside. Everything still smelled the same. The scent of fresh bread cooking caused me to rush into the kitchen. I am blessed through my pregnancy because I don't have morning sickness. *Knock on wood.* I rushed into the massive kitchen and Jolen was cooking just as I thought. The sight of me rushing inside startled her, but when she realized it was me, she stretched her arms wide with tears welling in her eyes.

"I just knew you were coming back. I prayed every day, and I knew that you would be back," she sobbed as she held me tight. I hugged her back for what seemed like hours. She pulled away from me, guiding me to a stool at the island.

"Tell me what finally brought you back."

"I came to talk to my parents. I have so many things I need to get off my chest."

"That you do. They are off in their usual places. Nothing has change, chile. But before you go, feed that baby," she said, giving me a knowing look that caused me to smile. "It's all over your face, the glow," she said, making me a huge bowl of chicken and dumplings.

Without a second thought, I snatched up the bowl and tore into it. Jolen is the woman who basically raised me. Her food is what I compare everyone else's to. I have many childhood memories and she is in them all. I guess I could consider her more of a mother than my real mom.

After I was done eating, she sat the entire pot aside for me including the French bread she was baking, and I had a huge smile on my face as I walked up the stairs to my father's study. Talking to him would be the easiest, even though emotionally it will be a challenge. Lightly tapping on his door, I eased inside. He looked up from his papers as if he was expecting someone else, but seeing me cause him to stand from his seat. I just stood there feeling uncomfortable. I suddenly wanted to rush back down the stairs and out of the house.

"You're here to stay." He said it more like a wish than a question. I could hear the longing in his voice.

"No, I'm just here to talk to you and mom. I need to get some things off my chest."

He gestured for me to join him over at his seating area, and I followed him and sat in the chair furthest from his seat. He seemed wounded by the gesture but didn't comment on it.

"So, what do we have to discuss?" I took a deep breath and pulled up the courage to have this conversation, finally.

"After Sheila's accident and Melissa's death, things around here just went back to the same. Well, in front of me you did. Everything was just back to business as usual. That was until, I heard what you and mom said that night before I left. I was heading to the kitchen when I heard the two of you arguing. I heard you tell her that you got her pregnant to give Jolen a child because she couldn't carry one for you. I heard you tell her that you wished Jolen was my mother and that I'm fucked up on the inside because I come from her." Tears streamed down my face as I poured it all out.

"You were never supposed to hear that."

"BUT IS IT TRUE? Did you get her pregnant to keep your mistress?" He hung his head low, and that told me everything I wanted to know.

"I forgive you, and I still love you. Even though it hurt me so bad to hear that, I still love you, daddy. I just wanted you and mom to love me back. To give me the love that I saw her give to you, which you then gave to Jolen. You guys thought that you could buy my love. You gave me everything that I could ever dream of, but you never taught me how to love or be loved.

Gosh, dad! I did so many things just to get you guys' attention, but it was never an issue. I was your *angel.* I was supposed to save two relationships, but all I did was become a pawn in your plots. You and mom taught me how to manipulate and how to use people for my own personal gain. I'm a murderer, and you made me this way."

"Angel, I've always loved you, and all these years I have watched you. I know that I was not a great father and I apologize for that, but if you would allow it, I will do my very best to make up for it. You are the only living piece of me, and I cannot fathom going another five years without hearing from you. Each day, I sit and hope that you would walk through those doors and today my wish was granted. Angel, I will do anything to be the father you deserve." Him saying that made me run over and jump into his arms. He hugged me tightly as I cried into his massive chest.

"I love you, daddy."

"I love you more, angel."

After sitting and talking with my daddy for a while, he told me that my mom wasn't in her best of minds. She has early onset Alzheimer's and is heading towards a decline. He led me to the room she was sleeping in, and I climbed into bed with her singing Nat King Cole's "Unforgettable". It's a song she would listen to for hours and hours when I was young. I would sit quietly by their bedpost and watch as she danced with her imaginary partner singing and smiling. Every day that she sang it, she would pause to stare me in the face and say, "I could never forget you, my sweet angel."

I've always known my mother was off at times, but that didn't cause me to love her any less. I just always wanted them to accept me and to make me feel like they truly wanted me.

"I could never forget you my, sweet angel," she cooed softly with a soft kiss to my forehead. I shot my head up to look in her face, and she had the biggest smile.

"I think we should dance, don't you?" I nodded my head, yes, and we stood to our feet dancing like the old days, except now I was her partner.

With a huge smile, I followed my beautiful mother's lead as she took me to her special place. This song was her way of letting me know that she would always try to remember me. It was her way of telling me that she truly loves me too even if she didn't effectively show it.

"Unforgettable, that's what you are
Unforgettable though near or far
Like a song of love that clings to me
How he thought of you does things to me
Never has been more
Unforgettable."

-Nat King Cole

Walking back into the house at midnight, I was on cloud nine. Shanty was so right. Talking to my parents was just what I needed, and it was such perfect timing. For the first time, I feel like I have that love I've been so desperately craving. It's such a powerful feeling. I opened the door to my room, and immediately I smelled his cologne. I was happy deep down, but I knew I had to remain strong. If I take him back, he will continue to do me the way that he does.

"Where you been?" he asked, sitting on the bed in his boxers, holding my sonogram picture from 2 days ago in his hand. He looked so damn good that I want to climb on top of him and let him take over my body the way he always does.

"I went to see my parents. Donavan, why are you here?" He just stared at me for a while like he wanted to know if I was lying or not. After a while, he dropped his stare and rubbed his head.

"I'm sleepy, and I can't sleep without you come here."

"Hell no! Get up and get out. I'm not doing this with you." Quickly he stood to his feet and pinned me up against the wall.

"You're pregnant with my baby, so that means you have to fucking be with me."

"In what world, Donavan? In what world should I just openly accept all the bullshit that you dish out without giving me anything good in return? You've never told me that you love me. You've never officially given us a title, and every time you get upset, you put your hands on me. I don't deserve any of this. Our child doesn't either."

"Why do I have to say all that if you know how I feel?"

"How would I know how you feel? The first time we had a disagreement you went and slept with another woman and came back nearly choking me to death." That caused him to get a look of guilt over his face.

"It was just fucking pussy."

"Would it just be dick if I slept with another man?"

He grabbed me by my throat and lifted me to his eye level. I clawed at his hands, kicking and fighting, and he quickly let me go rushing away from me pacing the floor.

"I don't know what to do," he said as he sat on the bed, looking at his hands. "I don't want you to leave me. I need you Malaika, but I don't know what to do." I walked up to him and pulled him towards me. He wrapped his arms around my waist with his head was flat against my stomach.

"You have to work on dealing with your issues. You need to let the past go so that we can move forward. I want to be with you, but not if you're going to treat me like shit. So, whatever ever issues you have with women needs to be resolve if we are going to have a future together." He clutched me tighter, and I rubbed his head singing softly to him. He has to let it all go if we ever have a chance of a future. Whatever demons he's holding on to he needs to let them go or else we can never be together again.

TWENTY-ONE

Trouble

"Look, bitch. Can you fix me or not?"

"Mr. Troy, for the last time I will not have you referring to me in that manner. Now, I know you have issues, but in order for me to help you, I need you to open up. I am a relationship therapist not a psychic. I cannot read your mind and magically "fix you".

This is the fifth fucking therapist, and I'm ready to lay hands on this bitch too. All these motherfuckers want me to come out and tell them shit that doesn't even matter. What the fuck does my childhood got to do with me wanting to be with Malaika? Fuck this shit I'm just about to go kidnap Malaika's ass and lock her back up. This shit is stupid and Ice a fucking duck for suggesting it.

"Mr. Troy, I know that you have your reservations about doing this, but I assure you that if we get to the root of your problem, we can most definitely get you where you want to be with Malaika. If you truly care for her, you will at least try. I'm licensed in hypnotherapy, and it has proven to work for my clients who aren't ready to willingly dive into the past. I can take you back to any place internally and it will allow you to recall the memories. It will be like you're reliving the moments and feeling the exact feelings you felt. It is intense, but it pays off tremendously."

"Whatever, bitch; the shit just better work."

"Mr. Troy, could you please refrain from using derogatory terms with me."

"Bitch, for the money I'm paying, I can whip my dick out and slap your edges back on. Shut the fuck up and swing the fucking watch so that I can get fixed and get my woman back. Ian trying to listen to yo wannabe white ass mouth no fucking more, anyways."

She gave me a look, but for $300 an hour, the bitch knew better. Shit, she's looking like she wants me to slap her on the head with my dick for real.

"Well, let's move over to the sofa, shall we?" I got up and followed her over, lying back on the chaise lounge chair.

"Okay, Mr. Troy. I want you to take long deep breaths. Yes, that's right, and each time I want you to relax on the exhale. Completely let go. Feel yourself slipping further and further from consciousness. Your body should be floating, are your floating?"

"Bitch, does it look to you like I'm floating?"

"You have to stop fighting the process, Mr. Troy! Clear your head completely. Take long deep breaths, releasing control as you slip further and further." Doing as she said I felt myself floating. My body felt lifeless as I eased between being conscious and unconscious.

"Now think of a happy place, in this place you are completely happy and stress-free. Are you there?"

"Yes?"

"Where are you, Mr. Troy?"

"I'm at home with Malaika."

"What are you doing?"

"We're lying in bed. I'm asleep, and she's singing to me while rubbing my head."

"Hang on to that and let her voice put you further and further at ease. Are you there?"

"Yes."

"Now, let's go back to the day it all started. Don't think your self-conscious will automatic guide you to the right moment."

"I'm here."

"Now tell me all about it."

I walked quietly behind ma in my beat-up Batman shoes that didn't light up anymore. I had on one of my daddy's big t-shirts with a few holes in it, and it had syrup stains on the front from three days ago, plus a ketchup stain from last night. My once khaki pants were a pale light brown with dirt and food stains covering them. That didn't stop me from having to still wear them to school though. We didn't have the best, but my daddy told me if I do good in school and work hard after helping folks that one day I can take us out of our ran down section eight apartment. That's why every day I took all the stupid stuff them kids say because I know one day I'm gone be better than all them niggas. They care about stupid stuff like new Jordan's and Dickie pants, but I'm trying to grow up and buy old houses and fix them up.

Mama and I passed this one house every day. It's down a deep alleyway that's a shortcut to our apartments. It's big white, and it has a big porch that could fit a bunch of people. I could cook on the grill while my wife and kids sit on a wooden swing that I built with my bare hands. I could see my kids running around the lot on the side of the house playing while me and their mama watched. I would have my arm wrapped around her shoulder, and she would lay her head up against me. Every day I passed that house, I would see the same vision.

"Don, you hea me, boy?"

"When we go up in this sto don't you follow behind me ni. You stay down the candy aisle and wait, till I say fa you to come on. You want them Spiderman shoes this time?" she asked, and I just nodded.

I'm really too old to be wearing those types of shoes, and they always fit too little, but they were easier for my mama to steal cause she could hide them better. All the clothes and stuff I get comes from the dollar store.

"Isaac is already down to BP buying us some beers with my stamps. I told him to grab you some little chips and cookies. I'ma get some canned beans and noodles, and we gone be straight for a week. Yo greedy ass better not eat two packs in one day like you done last week. You getting too damn tall and greedy," she complained as we walked, and I didn't say nothing. She stopped a little ways off from the dollar store and turned to look at me.

My mama was average height, and I came up to her shoulders at only ten years old. She always says that one day she'll scrape up the money so I can play ball like I beg her to. She told me I got the height to be great, but she doesn't know I ball at the center with the older boys. It's one of the ways I earn a little bit of my respect back from 'em. I chew 'em up on the court, and they see that I got a little something going for me. She tilted my chin upwards so that I could look her in the eyes. Her eyes misted over, and I could tell what she was about to say was hard for her.

"Donovan, you the best thing I ever done. I want you to know that and to remember that. My mama warned me about running around with Isaac, but I was young and foolish," she scoffed with a shake of her head like she was in disbelief that grandma was right.

"I gave up a good living to run behind him, and I never regretted any of it, until I had you. I got on drugs with ya daddy when you was six months, and I haven't been able to kick that pipe since. I hear that Pippy calling me in my sleep and I gotta wake up to suck on 'em. Don, I'm messed up baby, but I need you to hea me and hea me good, ok." I nodded my head for her to continue.

"You gotta get a thicker skin about yo self. It's good that you smart but you a boy and this world don't care nothing about our kind as it is. This world gone chew you up if you don't learn to toughen up. If a boy comes up to you picking on you, beat his ass like you done to Isaac for hitting on me that time. I know you got that anger in ya baby, and its ok to let that out sometimes. Show people that you can't be walked over. I love you baby, and everything I do is for your good. You may not see it, but my reasons are all good." She kissed my cheek, and I smiled.

"Now when we go in here, you stay on the candy aisle like I told you and wait for me to come get you. No matter how long it takes just wait. Don't leave on yo own," she said, and I nodded my head. We walked the rest of the way to the store, and I went to the candy aisle, while she went on to steal for us.

A girl on the aisle looked at me with her nose turned up, and I know it's cause I smell bad. I stepped away from her and kept on pretending to be looking for candy. I waited for the longest time before I left the aisle to look for mama. I went to the clothes section, the household section, and even hygiene section. Mama was nowhere in the store. I figured maybe she got caught and had to leave the store in a hurry. She did that once before, and Isaac came up to get me.

"Hey there, do you need help with something?" a pretty white woman asked.

She had a button down shirt instead of a collared one, so I figured she was in charge.

"No," I said and walked off from her.

I went back to the aisle and waited on mama or Isaac to come back. More time past and I was just standing there doing what I was told. I don't like to make mama mad cause she'll get upset, and Isaac will step in, and I don't want to have to fight him again. I broke his nose last time, and it made mama cry. I hated seeing her cry like that. It hurt me so bad that I cried too.

"Hey young man, can you come with me for a second?" a police officer said, walking on the aisle.

The white woman probably called him. I should've just left and gone home by myself. I went with him without saying a word. He asked me all types of questions, but I never answered. Someone in the store recognized me and told him where I lived. I got a little mad cause I know mama will think it was me, but they left me up here so it more of their fault than mine.

The officer drove me to our raggedy apartment and knocked hard on the door, and it swung open. Our door was already broke cause a D boy kicked it in looking for his stuff Isaac stole last week. I haven't had time to fix it back yet. It's hard finding good wood around here. He walked inside, and it was dark and quiet. I ran into mama and Isaac's room, and it was empty. All that was in there was their bed, and their dresser had all the drawers handing out. Nothing was in the closet either. I ran to my room, and all my stuff was still there. I only had a twin mattress on the floor and a basket with my clothes in it.

"Son, I'm going to have to take you back down to the station. I've alerted Child Protective Services, and they are on their way. I'm sorry," he said, looking at me all sad like the way teachers do when they ask me about my clothes and shoes.

I shrugged it off and followed behind him like a lost puppy. Mama left me in the store and came to move all her stuff away. My feelings were hurt, but I wouldn't let no tears fall. I had to get tough like mama said.

I went down to the station; then the lady took me to a group home for the night. I ended up staying there for a while. Every day, I was waiting on mama to come get me like she said. I knew mama loves me, and she always makes a way for me, so I knew she was coming. Days turned into months, and after a year, I gave up hope. Fuck every nigga and every bitch; it's every man for himself.

"Okay, Mr. Troy. Come back now. Slowly pull yourself out while holding on to the vividness of your memory. Forgetting no details and feeling every emotion." As she said it, I came back, opening my eyes and staring up at the ceiling.

"Mr. Troy, I am extremely pleased with the progress we just made. I can say with certainty that in order for you to move forward and be a better man for Malaika, you will need to find your mother and get the answers you're searching for from her. You suffer from extreme abandonment issues, stemming from your mother leaving you in that store that day. Your degradation of women is a direct result of all of these issues. Finding your mother will help you to lay some of these issues to rest."

I closed my eyes and took everything the bitch was saying in. The one thing she wants me to do is the same shit I've been avoiding for years. I've always wanted to find my bitch of a mother, but not to get answers. I wanted to find her and that fuck nigga she calls my daddy to put a bullet in both of their heads. I'll go ahead and find the bitch, but I can't promise she'll be breathing after I do.

TWENTY-TWO

Shanty

"You can't fucking do this! I'm a good mother! Wait! Wait! Please!"

I just stood there staring at this bitch putting on a show. I've been a social worker long enough to tell the difference between real reactions and fake ones. She's doing all this carrying on when I've given her ample warnings. She knows for a fact that her boyfriend has a no-contact order out for their daughter, yet she still had him around. I won't even get into why the bitch would want to be with a man who broke her daughter's leg— a fucking one-year-old at that. My heart shattered when I got to the hospital and saw that baby lying there so helpless and in pain. I wanted to take her right then, but there were protocols, and she wasn't at the house when the shit happened.

"Ma'am, I have given you the paperwork. Your hearing is on Friday; that is the place for you to plead your case. We have the signed order or removal, and we have to do our jobs," I stated that shit as kindly as I could while praying that the bitch would move her stank breath as out my damn face. It's twenty minutes to five, and it took all damn day just to get a judge that wasn't in court.

"Bitch, you gone give me my fucking baby!" she shouted, flipping the script. This bitch must have seen the labels on me and thought I wasn't from the hood cause she ran up on me.

Ion give a fuck about no damn regulations and protocols. Ain't no bitch running up to swing on me period. As soon as she cocked her hand back to swing, I laid her ass out then walked off with the officer and her baby.

She can say whatever she wants in court, but I got a sworn officer of the law on my side. That bitch should have taken her musty feet ass in the house instead of running up. As we were pulling up to the office, my phone started to ring. I asked the officer to take the child inside while I took the call because it was Neron's mama. She was probably planning some big ignorant ass dinner and begging me to get him to come like she did two weeks ago.

"Hello?"

"Oh Shantalya, you must get down here at once. Something has happened to my son; he's in critical condition." Not even bothering to hear the rest, I hung up and ran to my car.

Calling my boss on my headset I explaint to her that my husband was in the hospital, she agreed to take over the case and place the child for me, and I was so thankful. I got to the hospital in record time and rushed to the ICU. The nurse showed me to the room as the doctor was coming our way.

"Dr. Hill, This is Mrs. Avery." The look the doctor gave me wasn't a good one. Something bad was wrong with Neron, and I just knew it in my soul. Whatever it is we will pull through it. I know that we will.

"Mrs. Avery, when your husband arrived here with his mother he had already been without oxygen for some time. The CPR and other things just simply could not make up for that. Though we were able to bring him back, he may never wake up. In the event that he does there will be substantive cognitive, motor, and speech impairments."

"Wha-what are you t-t-trying to say?" I felt like I got hit by a freight train as he spoke. I knew what he meant, but I just couldn't understand it. Everything was happening so fast.

"Your husband is brain dead."

Brain dead, brain dead, brain dead! I know that he said it once, but those words just kept echoing through my head as the room started to spin. Everything was just too surreal. Hours ago, we were having sex at the breakfast table. He was just texting me saying he loved one my lunch break. How could he just be gone so soon? We just got married. It's only been three months. We are still newlyweds; we haven't had enough time.

"Take me to him," I spoke through my chaotic thoughts.

They took me to his bedside, and I was horrified looking at him hooked up to all those machines. Everything the doctors said finally click. They violated his rights. I grew angry watching his mother clutching his hand crying. She knew he didn't fucking want this.

"Who authorized this?" I shouted.

"To what are you referring to?"

"I'm referring to the fact that he had a DNR, and you have him hook up to all this shit, and you openly admitted to someone performing CPR on him. I suggest you fucking unhook him, or I will sue the fuck outta every damn body who laid hands on him!"

The doctor rushed over to grab his chart, and when he did, he went pale as a ghost. He knew they fucked up. His mother was busy staring a hole into the side of my head, but I didn't give a fuck. The doctor quickly unhooked Neron from all the machines, and I waited for him to take his last breath before I stormed out of the hospital. I passed his siblings on the way out, but I had no words for them.

"Mrs. Avery!" Trevor called. I turned around to look at him.

"This is from Mr. Avery," he said handing me an envelope then turning to walk away.

This is the one time I'm thankful that he is overly professional. I don't think I can handle an I'm sorry or a hug right now. I rushed into the elevator and down to my car. I eased into my car with the note in my hand. Turning the car on, "Why I Love You" by MAJOR was playing softly through the speakers. Mustering up the courage, I opened the letter from Neron.

Love,

If you're reading this, then it means my time has come. I sat awake so many nights pondering the ways that I could tell you, but it was an unbearable task. I was diagnosed with an inoperable brain tumor, on that very day that we met. I was sitting in the mall watching people pass me by when I looked up to see the most beautiful woman I ever laid eyes on. Looking at you, I could see the defeat radiating from your body. I saw your insecurities, your pain, and the longing in your heart for love. It was then that I knew that I wanted to give my dying breath, breathing life back into you.

Love, I've known from the start that you could never fully love me, but that didn't cloud my love for you. Loving you was the greatest joy of my existence. You made dying the best and the worst experience. I prayed to the heavens for more time. I prayed that time could stand still and I could just hold you in my arms for eternity, but you were never mine. Our love was necessary for your growth, but we were not meant to be. Your heart was already promised to another.

Don't fret love; I bare no regrets. Giving the opportunity again, I wouldn't dare to change a thing. I love you, Shantalya, and I will love you or an eternity in the afterlife. Go on and live your life. Smile, my love. You know I hate to see those tears. Do all the things that your heart desires knowing that tomorrow is not promised. All that was mine is now yours. Keep my memory alive and always cherish the special moments, because the best come once in a lifetime.

With love, always, Neron

Tears poured from my eyes as I sat letting everything soak in. He loved me knowing that he could never have all of me. He was willing to sacrifice that for me. As everything hit me, I threw the car in drive heading towards my happiness. *Do all the things that your heart desires knowing that tomorrow is not promised.*

"I will baby! I will," I said, smiling through the tears. I pulled in outside of the house hopping out of the car. My nerves were in a frenzy as I banged on the door.

"Yo who the fuck—" seeing me stopped his rant.

"I want us back! I want you to be the man that I die loving," I said as a new wave of tears poured down my face. Fame grabbed me pulling me into his arms kissing me passionately. Picking me up, he carried me to the bedroom still kissing me deeply. Laying me on the bed, he stared into my eyes.

"Shanty, I'll never hurt you again. I'm going to spend the rest of my life proving that I'm that man for you," he said with a tear slipping for his eye. Reaching up, I wiped the tear pulling him down to me. Slow but urgently we undressed while still locked in our passionate kiss. He entered me, causing my back to arch off the bed.

"I fucking missed you," he whispered into my ear as he eased in and out of me. I wrapped my arms around him, pulling him closer to me. I wanted to feel him to know that he's real.

"Don't ever hurt me again," I cried on the verge of an orgasm.

"I won't," he said, kissing me again. I threw my head back and allowed him to make love to me. With every stroke, he wiped the doubt from my heart, replacing it with affirmations of his love. Fame wasn't the same man as he was months ago. He's better; he's the missing piece that I've been longing for. This time I know that we will last forever.

TWENTY-THREE

Ice

I sat at the desk kicking my feet up, unbuttoning my suit jacket for extra comfort. I took the liberty of going through the nigga's drawers and shit. I was just making myself at home in this nigga little box size office. I never pegged Archie for the stupid type, but this nigga got one hundred thousand and up cars in his driveway, and his office looks like a fucking closet. How the fuck he thought he could fucking take my spot when he can't even look up and see the bottom of my feet.

Me and Gip had been following that nigga on different rotations, and I pretty much know that nigga is the last link. Trouble already told me that he found Archie's numbers in the two niggas from Lai's apartment phones. That nigga called himself running shit, but got coke heads and crazy niggas on his team. My pride was slick hurt on that shit cause in a way maybe that fuck nigga got it in his head that I'm an easy target. Just cause I got my head on my shoulders don't mean I can't nut up like my brothers. The alarm beeping alerted me that the nigga is finally coming in. About fucking time. The nigga rushed in with his gun drawn, and I couldn't help but fall over in laughter.

"Damn nigga, I almost blasted your ass." I had tears coming

down at this point. I laughed straight up until he joined in. The shit immediately stopped being funny. I hit that Kanye laugh on that nigga real quick.

"What you doing here? You got some shit you need me to handle?"

"Nah, I'm here to handle some shit personally. You know to tie up loose ends and all that shit."

"Loose ends?" He had the nerve to fake a laugh like he ain't know what I was talking about.

"You know why I picked to do this shit here and not in your car or outside that nigga you're working against me for crib?" His response was an uneasy head nod.

"Because I believe that those we cared for should be buried with honor. I want someone to find you so that your mother can come and bury you decently. I'm a firm believer in Karma."

"If you believed in that you wouldn't be here to kill me."

"Every man's day shall come. This is your day and mine will come too. Maybe soon maybe later, who knows. Nevertheless, my karma would be being buried honorably as I have every life that I take. I didn't force you to cross me. You could have come to me for anything, bro. I started with branching out with three fucking bricks. I got rid of that shit in half the time and brought you niggas on to make more moves. I fucking did that shit, not you. You want to be the fucking boss, but you ain't never stood under fire for this shit. I did. It's my fucking money and my brother backing me up that got me started up."

"I was there for all that shit too."

"Asking for a fucking handout! You a bitch ass nigga and ian even bothering with the back and forth. You crossed the one motherfucker that would have handed you this shit. A nigga's thinking about retiring before I hit thirty. This shit could have been all you nigga but you ain't built the right way. You slither and slide behind motherfucker's back threatening women and kids for fucking money. The only thing you're loyal to is the dollar and ian never seen one of them niggas jump off a green bill to save a nigga. How many bullets did it take for you though, BRO? You know what, fuck the shit." I pulled my gun and sent one through his skull; no longer in the mood to even give this nigga any more of my fucking time or energy.

I walked up to his body and double tapped, sealing the deal before creeping back out the basement window that leads out back. When I go back to my car, I just sat back and thought about every fucking thing. This street shit is getting old. When your day one niggas start flipping for paper, it's time to start moving towards the legit route. Niggas ain't built right no more.

~

I sat in my man cave with Fame killing that nigga in Call of Duty. That nigga got mad and quit on 2k. He been on some extra shit since we found out Mama Rosemary with Big Dee. I was against it too, but when she explained how much she loves the nigga and how good he treats her what more could I say. Trouble, ain't really fucking with them being together, but lately, he been off doing his own shit. The nigga is probably plotting on how to kidnap Lai and disappear.

"Ice!" Niyah called out with lil dude on her hip like a fucking baby.

"Put him down, Ni. He's fucking seven; you gone handicap him. Lil dude, come play the game and help me beat Uncle Fame." He jumped from Niyah's arms, and of course, she was rolling her eyes and shit.

"I came in here to tell you that you have company. I'll just send them back here and since I'm handicapping him, watch him while I go help Shanty make arrangements for Neron's funeral. It would be considerate for you to fucking call her and at least act like you feel sympathy for her!" she snapped, and I just ignored her loud mouth ass. If it's nothing important, I don't talk to her ass.

"Nigga, you in the dog house like a motherfucker. Oh my fault, sup lil' man," Deuce said walking into the den and sitting over on the vacant couch.

"Ian in shit; her ass is on my bad side. Where's your wifey?"

"In there talking shit with yours. Fame nigga, I heard about ole boy dying. You in the good now, ain't it?" Deuce asked and Fame shook his head.

"Let's go talk in the other room," I said, and we all got up heading into the den down the hall. Niyah was standing in the foyer with Rina talking shit. Her loud mouth was going a mile a minute as her arms and hair swayed as she emphasized every fucking word.

"Bro, she's on yo ass," Fame laughed, and I shook my head as we all sat down around the circular layout of the furniture.

"Man, so Shanty shows up to my door, crying telling me she's ready for us and all that. Then we go upstairs and bro! I had to just look at her and hold her close to make sure it wasn't one of my fucking dreams cause I been dreaming about her ass nonstop. The shit was all real, and she had me feeling sparks like a lil bitch or something. I'm a grown ass man lying in bed fucking getting goosebumps, bro. That shit was the best ever, in life my nigga.

In all the times I fucked a bitch or fucked her, that time she had me on some female type of shit. I'm lying in bed holding her close so she won't dip out. That shit didn't work cause I woke up to an empty bed. The only way I knew it really happened was cause she took some of my sweats and left her clothes. I've been on some creep shit, sniffing her panty every day."

"Nigga, you could have kept that shit to yourself." I said feeling disgusted as fuck.

"Ion blame him though fam. I would be on the same shit," Deuce said, causing us all to laugh. A while later Rina finally walked in telling me that Ni took lil dude, which I knew she was. She doesn't ever go nowhere without him right by her side. I gotta fight to even watch cartoon with my lil dude around her ass. Fame and I extended our condolences for Big Sy's passing and after we paid respect with a moment of silence we got down to business.

"So, since you guys are family. I dug DEEEEP and the information I got for y'all is juicy!" Rina exaggerated, and we all just looked at her waiting for her to tell us what the fuck was up.

"So, it all starts back in '91 when Markus Stinger was first joining the force. Within his first week, he was suspended due to corruption, but that's not juicy so let me skip along. Markus Stinger's father is Marks!"

"OG pimp, hoe selling extraordinaire Marks?" Fame said, causing us all to laugh. That nigga ain't have to add all that extra shit.

"Yes, the very same. So, apparently, he let Markus join the force so he could someday gain the ranks and have the best of both worlds. Well on that day that Markus was suspended, he went to his father agreeing to take on the family business. Well, Marks is famous for his insurance policies. Everyone who joins has to prove themselves by committing a crime for him, like a gang initiation. That night with Markus was no different. Marks had his men take him out to go and rape a Hispanic girl. Are you following?" We all nodded yes, and she continued.

"That same night Markus also got close to one of his father and now his girls. He forced her to quit hooking, and she became his side bitch, and they actually fell in love. Well, over time she got tired of the same ole shit with him. He was basically controlling her entire life while he lived happily with his wife. By now, she and he had a baby, and she was ready to pack their things and runoff. Seeing that she was pulling away, the story is that Markus started giving her crack to keep her on a leash, basically turning her into an addict for the drugs and for him."

"That's a cool and slightly boring little story, but what's that got to do with us?" Fame blurted.

"Well, the girl that he raped showed up to the station with a huge belly as proof that an officer in uniform raped her. Although the case never saw the light of day the girl still had his baby in hope that someday she would get justice."

"So, this nigga got two kids out there somewhere?" I asked in confusion still not putting the shit together. This nigga is mad at us because he was a dirty cop and a half-ass pimp?

"Two sons were born to Ignacia Esperilla and Denise Johnson." Fame and I just stared at each other when she said that shit. "You two are real brothers."

My fucking mind was blown. On one end, I'm happy as fuck

that we blood. Shit, if Trouble ended up being blood too, the shit would be even better, but what the fuck does us being his son got to do with him plotting to kill us.

"So, our father is trying to off us?" Fame asked. I looked over, and Deuce was just staring on like he was watching a movie. Hell, this is some crazy ass shit.

"Before he died, Marks found out about you two. He wrote it in his will that the two of you were to take over the business when the youngest son turns 25. Fame's birthday is coming up, and Markus knows that rightfully he must step down so that you two can take over the family business. His motive is greed pure and simple. He wants everything for himself."

"And in the end, that will leave the nigga with nothing. I will see to that." I barked sitting back thinking. My gears were turning. It's time to take this nigga out and put this all to rest. Shit, right now I wish I were fucking with Ni for real cause I need to lay under her and rest my mind.

TWENTY-FOUR

Niyah

You would think that since I have Anju and Ice killed Archie that he would start trying to work on us. I mean that makes the most damn sense, right? Especially since the nigga still got me living up in here and walks around bonding with my son like we're a big happy family. Well, if you thought that shit bitch you thought wrong! That nigga doesn't pay me no damn mind. If it's not absolutely necessary, he doesn't address me. He sleeps in the master bedroom, and I sleep in a guest room with Anju. At first, the shit didn't bother me because I was bonding with my son, but now he has taken this shit too fucking far. It's been months, and I'm sick of his bullshit, but I got something for his ass.

He thinks I don't know that he been out at strip club with Gip. I am not fucking stupid. I got too many eyes in that club to not know when my man steps foot into that bitch. So, since he likes going to strip clubs to watch strippers, I figured I'd bring this ass out of retirement. I keep saying this ain't no fucking Trouble and Malaika type of relationship. I know how to get ignorant right the fuck back. Ice is not about to play this mind game shit with me.

I finished packing an overnight bag for Anju and grabbed him careful not to wake him up. After slinging the bag over my shoulder,

I headed down to my car. I put him in his booster seat and buckled him down before getting in my car and heading to Mama Rosemary's house. Shanty and Lai will be watching him for me tonight. I know Lai will mostly have him because Shanty has been in a sleep coma since Neron died three days ago. Lai and I've been by her side every step of the way, and I hate to not be there tonight, but I gotta get my nigga in check.

If anything Neron dying has taught us all is that life is too damn short to let bullshit get in the way. I'm about to teach Ice this one good lesson, and hopefully, he'll learn to stop playing games with a player. His ass thinks he's the master manipulator, but I keep telling muh'fackas ain't no man got shit on a fed up woman. Parking behind Shanty's car, I got out getting Anju and his bag out. Walking in the house, I could hear Lai on her guitar playing something peaceful. As I got up the stairs, I could hear that it was a song she wrote.

"Is she up?" I asked, easing on inside the room. Lai, Mama Rosemary, and Shanty were all in bed. Instantly I started to feel bad. This shit with Ice can wait until another time. I need to be here for my friend. Laying Anju down on an empty spot on the huge king size bed, I climbed in kicking off my shoes.

"I thought you were going to handle things with Ice?" Lai whispered still strumming softly on her guitar.

"That can wait; I need to be here for my girl right now."

"Niyah, take your ass and go get your damn man. I'll still be here tomorrow, and Neron will still be gone. I know that you care and that you want to be here and that all matters, but take your ass down to that strip club and drag your unhappy man up out of there from around them vultures." Shanty said with her eyes still closed.

"You sure?"

"Bitch, if you don't hurry up you gone surely be single." She popped up in the bed on my ass and I knew she was serious. I just laughed at her and rushed out racing to the club. Pulling up outside, I grabbed my bag and headed inside. It's time to liven shit up in this bitch.

"How's everybody doing up in here tonight! Yeeeaaaaa! We're gone liven things up in this bitch. I need everybody on ya fucking feet money in hand. Don't throw no fucking ones on the stage! The lady I got coming up is top notch!"

"Nigga, spin my shit!" I said over the mic I had taped to my face. I'm in this bitch with the Beyoncé mic set cause I got some shit to say while I shake my ass.

"I got you, baby." He did a quick spin before playing "Rake It Up" by Yo Gotti.

On my cue, I made my way to the stage ass naked. Damn right. I know Ice ain't gone give me a chance to dance for real, so I started with no clothes on. I walked up to the pole and dance around not even bothering to look up for Ice cause I know he's on his way down. After doing a little tease, I turned around facing the crowd.

"Who trying to go home with Purrfection tonight?" Nigga's went crazy trying to reach out for me as I stared at them with a huge smile.

"Ohh what's your name, baby? You look like you trying to take me home tonight."

I was flirting with this fine ass nigga in the crowd. He mouthed his name before reaching out to me, but I couldn't even do shit else because I was snatched off the stage. He used his shirt to cover my naked body, and I inhaled the scent of his Clive Christian cologne. His body was stiff and rigid as he carried me through the club and out to his red Maserati, tossing me inside.

He got in still not saying a word. I didn't even get the chance to ask about my shit because before I could, Gip was coming out with everything. Ice rolled the window down letting him toss everything in before driving off.

We pulled up to the house, and he just sat there still not saying shit. I got out of the car, and he followed suit. I thought for sure he was gone light into my ass as soon as we hit the door, but he didn't. See now this shit is pissing me the fuck off. These little mind games and shit he knows damn well he's mad that the whole club, including his right-hand, saw my pretty, bare pussy. He tried brushing past me going up the stairs, but I grabbed his arm.

"Nigga, what the fuck is wrong with you?" He just snatched his arm away laughing at me as I fell down.

Oh, now shit is about to get real cause he got me fucked up. Hopping up, I ran up the stairs meeting the back of his head with harsh blows. He managed to turn around and get a grip on my arms pinning me to the side of our spiral staircase. I was still struggling to get free so that I could fuck his ass up until he gave me a hard ass slap to the face. My left ear was ringing, and my face was hot and throbbing.

"Chill the fuck out before I beat your ass. You mad cause ian playing into that hoe ass shit you pulled tonight. Ni, cool off on me before I beat the black out of your ass and have you spitting that Ching Chow Chung shit." Just as he said that I started cursing him straight the fuck off in Korean, calling him all types of dumb and stupid bitches. He wrapped his hands around my neck and squeezed.

"You got me fucked up if you think you gone call me another bitch. Don't look fucking surprised. I made it my business to starting learning Korean so that I can know what the fuck your sneaky ass be saying. Ion fucking trust you, so I need to understand every fucking word that leaves you lips and every move you fucking make. You pulling hoe ass stunts trying to get to me when all you doing is showing me I chose right in not trusting you. I never judge you for stripping or for that side shit you had going, but I see now I should have.

I should have never fucked with a scummy ass cum bucket bitch in the first fucking place. Then I would be so fucking miserable. Every time I look at you I want to lay you the fuck out. For crossing me, walking in my office ass naked, and now this shit. You think I want to stick my dick in or lay next to a bitch with no fucking morals. You don't fucking know how to carry yourself as a fucking lady. All this extra shit you been on don't fucking move me. I won't react to that simple-minded shit. You want my attention, try being a fucking lady and remembering that you have a fucking son."

He released my neck and walked away from me like I wasn't shit to him. I was so hurt that I just say my ass on the step and cried rocking myself slowly. I don't know what to do to get him to love me again.

~

I pulled up to the expensive over the top as funeral home right behind Neron's mama. Her driver opened the back door and she stepped out like the damn funeral was today. Head held upwards to the sky with her huge funeral hat with the veil shielding her face. She had on a bad as black dress that I knew cost twenty thousand easily. Her heels were something exclusive, and the old bitch was just bad. Grabbing my Chanel bag, I got out of my car shutting the door with confidence even though I felt so insecure inside.

"So, you just came up here to stir up more shit, I see!" Mama Rosemary spat, looking like she was a second from squaring up with Neron's mama. The poor little white man was turning bright red cause he knew it was about to go down.

"I came here to ensure that my son is laid to rest with tact. I know how you people bury your family, and I will not have any of that foolishness no. My son is to be laid in our family's vault like every other Avery."

Before Shanty or anyone else could reply, they saw me, and their mouths dropped open. Last night after everything that happened with Ice, I started thinking, and he was absolutely right. I do need to carry myself better. I walk around half-naked all the time, with my crazy nails, and bleach blonde hair to my ass. That isn't who I want my son to know me as and furthermore if my man is against it, I'm woman enough to let that shit go to better our relationship. I would be crazy to let small shit like that get in the way of our happiness. So, I went to the salon this morning and got a trim and dyed my hair back black. After that, I went shopping for a new wardrobe.

After all the trouble I went through, he had better act right, or I'm cutting the fuck up.

"You look so good Niyah," Lai said.

"I know the world is coming to an end when this chile waltz in looking like she ready to walk in a church fashion show." I laughed so hard at Mama Rosemary that my sides hurt.

"I'm just playing, chile. You look good as hell, keep it up."

"Mr. Sims, here are the papers my husband had drawn before his death. This is a strict guideline to how HE wanted everything to go. I expect it to be followed to the T because if you allow this woman to sway things in any way, I will sue the fuck out of you. I'm tired and grieving, so I don't have time to play tug of war with anybody. I'm his wife I have final say, so I don't even know why you're even here, Nuru!" Shanty spat, taking her attention from the mortician to focus solely on her. Shanty looked like she was ready to lay Nuru the fuck out in here. I just want it to be known I'm tagging the fuck in. I know I'm changing, but it's still brand new to me.

"I won't keep doing this back and forth shit. Neron is gone, and I did what the fuck he wanted. I won't sit up here and let you try to push shit off on me in no way. When your son was living, I had to be nice and cordial to your sad stiff face ass, but bitch he is dead, and I don't have to have shit to do with you. After his funeral, stay the fuck from around me and my dealings. Now have a good day. Come on y'all let's go to get something to eat; I need a damn drink."

With that, we all followed Shanty out of the funeral home and headed to Golden Corral because Mama Rosemary kept going on about wanting to eat from a buffet. We laughed and talked the whole time, and it was nice seeing my girl up in good spirits. She doesn't show it, but I know she's hurting badly.

TWENTY-FIVE

Fame

I feel like a sucker for the shit I'm about to do. I swear I feel like I need to be zipping up a fucking dress instead of tying my tie cause I feel like a bitch. As much as I don't want to do this shit, I know I have to for Shanty. That nigga's death is hitting her hard, and I gotta be there for her no matter what I'm feeling. Slipping on my gold Audemars watch and my gold chain, I checked myself out one last time in the mirror. I grabbed my shades and headed out to the gravesite. This nigga wasn't having his shit at a church. He was just doing a little gravesite service then letting them drop him in the ground. I pulled up at the graveyard and parked behind Trouble. As I was easing out my ride, Ice was pulling in.

"Man, ian feeling this shit bro," Ice said, and all I could do was shake my head at him.

"I was going for some food at the repast, but the way this shit is set up, that shit gone be bland ass fuck. They're probably eat that fish egg shit. I bet this why that old bitch's face is shaped like a fish. Eating all them fish eggs and snails and shit," Trouble said, causing me and Ice to laugh.

"I know the fuck you niggas did not bring your asses over here to ruin this man's funeral. Where's the rest of them crazy niggas at?"

Niyah spat, looking around like Yir and Ju were gone pop out a bush or something.

I shook my head at her ass while looking her over, but not in no sexual way. She changed her hair and shit up, and it makes her look prettier. Her Korean features were standing out more, and sis was looking like a runway model. I know Ice is feeling that shit. He had better get right before somebody comes snatch her and have him looking like my ass. The nigga's gone feel hella stupid strolling up to his girl's husband funeral.

"We ain't on that shit. Where's my lil dude at?" Ice asked.

"He's over there with Mama Rosemary, Shanty, and Lai. You know your mama is not letting him out of her sight. She spoils him worse than me."

Before Ice could respond to her, that nigga bitch ass brothers walked our way making Ice move sis behind him instinctively. Ian never been a bitch, so I walked up to meet them niggas halfway. I came in peace, but it ain't nothing to set this bitch off.

"I'm going to have to ask you to leave," one of them niggas said, sounding like a straight fucking square.

I looked at my brothers, and we all laughed at the niggas pushing our way past they weak asses. Real niggas don't ask shit. He gone have to ask us to leave. That's the funniest shit I done heard in a minute.

"Tyrell, don't come up fucking this man funeral up," Mama fussed as we walked to the site. I threw my hands out signaling that I wasn't on no hot shit. She gave me a look before turning to sit back down, leaving a spot for me to sit next to Shanty.

"What are you doing here?" she asked. It was a question of surprise, not disrespect.

"I'm here to support you, I know this shit hard on you, and I got your back."

She stared at me for a while then broke down crying. I pulled her close to me and held her. I knew that's all she really needs right now. The service went by smooth, and I was surprised cause I know that his moms don't rock with Shanty like that. Maybe the old bitch was worried about how it would look if she said something.

Either way shit went smooth, and they buried the nigga with no complications. Ian gone front though it was a decent ass burial, but a nigga like me want to go out Viking style. Put my casket on a boat and kick me out to sea then light my shit on fire. That's how the fuck I want to go out. Say what the fuck you want, but you ain't ever gone catch a nigga going out stronger than my shit!

"Thanks for coming to the funeral, you didn't have to do that," Shanty said as I stood in the kitchen making a plate. Mama cooked for all of us like the repast shit was over here. Nobody went to that fuck shit that nigga's peoples were having, not even Shanty.

"I owe you that much. Look, I know you not ready for us to get back right now, but that doesn't mean I can't be here for you. Ian gone trip out on you if you just show up to the house to kick it. Shit, if you just need to come sleep with me like the old days, I'm good on that, too. I'm on your timing Shanty, and I can wait forever if it takes that." She just stared at me for a while before nodding her head.

"Thanks."

I had so much shit that I wanted to say but couldn't. Seeing her standing here looking so fucking hurt did some shit to me inside, and I was happy that Trouble came in the kitchen breaking up the awkward ass moment.

"My bad; I came to fix Lai and my baby a plate."

"Somebody please come carry this nigga to the nut house. Lai's three days pregnant and this nigga talking about his baby like he got a toddler or some shit," I said to Shanty, making her laugh.

"Nigga, fuck you; she's eating for two."

"And you're thinking for three, overworked brain having ass nigga."

"Yo, fuck outta my face before I knock yo ass out."

"Nigga, lower your fucking voice before mama comes in here with that fucking back scratcher," I gritted.

We heard screaming and hollering making us all run up the

stairs. We got up there, and mama was beating the breaks off Niyah and Ice. We all sat back laughing at them trying to cover their naked bodies with the bed covers.

"I told yo ass about fucking in my damn house! I'm the only motherfucker that gets dicked down in my shit!" she hollered, alternating licks between them.

"We didn't do anything yet!" Ice yelled. He was doing his best to cover Niyah, but she was still catching licks.

"Oh, y'all want to watch. Come on in here; I got some more for all y'all asses too."

With that shit, we all hauled ass back down the stairs. She had me so fucked up about that shit, that I got in my car in left. I'll holler at everybody later. Ice gotta get up with me about that Markus nigga anyways.

~

I was sitting out in my back in my garage restoring my 1965 Ford Shelby Mustang GT350 when someone buzzed my gate causing my phone to go off. I just hit the button not even bothering to check who it was. Ice was the only nigga that supposed to be coming by here today, so I know it's him.

"Damn, she's getting closer and closer," Big Dee said, causing me to spin around fast as fuck.

"Nigga, the fuck you doing here?"

"Cool it, fam. I came to talk brother to brother."

"You ain't a brother of mine, nigga. Say yo peace so you can leave my crib." He sat on my rolling stool like he had some heavy shit on his mind. I propped my forearms on my car leaning over to look at him, just waiting for the nigga to say what he's gotta say.

"Ian never gave a fuck about beefing with no nigga. My whole life it's been get it how you live with me. I make my decisions, and I stand by that shit. You know what I mean?" He looked up at me like he wanted me to agree, but I wasn't with that shit. I just continued to stare at him. He chuckled and nodded his head.

"I know this shit with me and Rose is fucked up. Bro, I never wanted the shit to happen. It's like one minute she was making me a to-go plate and the next we were fucking. The shit happened just that damn fast, and I was ready to tell you off the rip, but she asked me not to. Shit, she begged me not to, so I let it just be between us. I wouldn't never fuck with her on some weak shit, bro. On everything, I really love Rose. She's the first woman that's got my nose wide open. Man, you know how she is, bro. She be having me together on my shit, and I can't even imagine my life without her in it."

"Nigga, I told her that I wasn't sweating what you got going. Why the fuck are you over here professing your love for her to me?"

"Because I want to marry her." I had to shake my head cause I was having one of those crazy dreams like the one I have about Shanty. Ain't no way my nigga my fucking right hand is coming over here telling me he's trying to wife my mama.

"Say what?" He stood up and pulled out a ring box opening it to show a huge ass ring. At least this nigga cashing her the fuck out.

"Big Dee, I just said I told mama that I wasn't tripping off what y'all got going, so again, what are you doing over here?"

"You told her you ain't tripping off us, but that ain't the same as giving her your blessing. Shit with us been has mad different since that day we fell out. She's hurting bro and man to man I had to come sit down with you. We can put this shit behind us. For her sake, even if we can never be brothers again, at least be there and show her that you love her enough to let this shit go."

"Nigga, I should shoot your bitch ass in the face," I gritted.

"Save that shit, nigga!" he spat back as I pulled him into a dap hug.

"You still a hoe ass nigga for fucking my mama, bro. But she got yo ass out here about to cry and shit if I don't give this shit my approval, so I can rock with it. Just don't fuck my mama over nigga. On God, one argument I hear about and I'm shooting you bitch ass in the eye socket."

"That's fair."

"Yea whatever. Grab a jumpsuit and help me finish fixing Roxanne up."

He grabbed the jumpsuit slipping it on, and we worked on my

car until Ice showed up to tell me what I already knew. The nigga Markus was in the wind, and that shit is Ice's fault for playing patty cake instead of killing muh'fuckas. Ian even too hot with the nigga cause I should have went ahead and killed that nigga myself. All I know is I'm bussing straight off the rip the next time the opportunity comes.

Fuck all that talking shit. I could care less why a muh'fucka wants me dead. As long as I kill his ass, his reasoning can die with him. That nigga can hide all he wants I know he gone pop back up soon cause my birthday coming around soon. When that nigga peeps his head out, I'm bussing it wide open like whack a mole. After Ice and Big Dee left, I took a quick shower and got in the bed ready to call the cows until the fucking bell rang. I hopped outta bed knowing it was Ice because he got stuck behind the fucking gate. I was surprised as fuck to see Shanty standing there.

"You said I could come to sleep like the old times."

Moving aside, I allowed her to come in, and without saying anything more, we got in bed in our underwear to go to sleep. We had distance between us at first, but I woke up to her crying in her sleep, so I pulled her close to me holding her tight. Holding on to her body had my heart feeling big as a motherfucker. I got her back for now, and all I gotta do is prove that I won't fuck up to keep her.

TWENTY-SIX

Shanty

I felt Fame lightly nudging me awake, and I slowly opened my eyes. He was standing beside the bed fully dressed, holding a tray of breakfast. I had to rub my eyes to make sure that I wasn't tripping. The Fame I know doesn't fucking cook.

"Who cooked this?"

"I did."

"Since when do you cook?"

"Come on, Shanty. We grew up in the same house, so you know mama taught us all how to cook. You did all the cooking, so I never had to do shit. You hungry or what?"

Sitting up, I grabbed the tray and started eating. It was good as hell; I should have made his ass cook some damn time back then.

"I gotta go handle some shit at the shop. I left a key on the nightstand, and you know the gate code so you can just come and go whenever you feel like it. Set the alarm with the same code you used to get in here, but with a two instead of four." He rambled that shit off so fast I could barely keep up.

"You heard me?"

"Yea."

"I'ight love you I'm out." I didn't respond I just let him leave. I'm starting to feel guilty again, and it was either him leaving or me. The first time I came over here, and we had sex, I felt so damn bad when I woke up in the middle of the night. My damn husband had just died, and the first thing I did was run back to Fame and fuck him. I owe Neron more than that. I feel like I cheated on him in a way. I don't know why my emotions are all over the place.

His lawyers are reading his will back at the house later, and I don't even want to go. I don't care what he left to who. Honestly, he could have left it all to fucking charity. I just don't even want to have to deal with any of it right now. His bitch ass mama gives me a fucking headache. I swear since he's been gone I've been wanting to drag that hoe down a concrete staircase. Just scrape all her shit the fuck up.

Finishing my breakfast and taking the orange juice to the head, I sat the tray down and made the bed back up before going to wash the dishes. Fame's ass hates washing dishes, so I know the sink is full. I was once again shocked because the kitchen was spotless. I started checking the trash cause I just knew his ass didn't cook and clean. I didn't find shit but proof that he did in fact cook. Shit, Fame really did get his shit together on my ass. I laughed at the thought as I head back up to shower and get ready. I ended up putting the clothes that I left over here from last time back on. He had it sitting on the dresser for me knowing that I was going to go through his clothes to find something if he didn't.

After thirty minutes of procrastinating, I finally put on my shoes and walked out of the door, making sure to set his alarm. I got into the car and headed over to my home that I haven't set foot in since Neron passed. Everything was starting to hit me harder and harder the closer I got to the neighborhood. I had to pull over to keep from crashing because I was so blinded by the tears. My phone buzzed in my purse, and I answered without looking.

"Calm down and stop crying," Fame instructed calmly. How the hell he knew I was crying is beyond me, but I'm beyond happy he called.

Fame always knows how to get me back on track. I just don't want to go back to that house and remember all the times we share.

I've been doing my best just to move forward and pretend, but going up in that house gone take me straight back. Thinking about everything made me cry even harder.

"Come on Shanty, man. You need me to come out there? Tell me what you need Shanty, and I'm on it."

"I don't want to do this; I can't go back there."

"Then turn around and go back to the house. I can pick you up some snacks and shit, and we can watch them movies you like or some shit. Whatever you want to do it's all on you, but eventually you gone have to face that shit head on. You just gotta dive in." The more he spoke, the more confidence I got, and I started my car and headed towards the house.

"If this goes bad, can we still eat snacks and watch movies?"

"Hell yeah, ion do shit but run my shops, sleep, and work on Roxanne every day. I'll take your company any way I can get it."

Laughing at his silly ass, I pulled into the dirt path leading to my home. The guard let me in immediately, and I parked in behind everyone else. I guess they all were eager to see how big their slice of the pie is.

"Stay on the phone."

"Shanty, you trying it now man. Can't you call Lai or Niyah loud ass? They live for shit like this."

"Fame, please just put your phone on mute and I'mma have you on speaker."

"Man, you lucky I love your ass or I'd demand some head for this shit!" he spat doing as I asked. I bet money he's still talking shit on the other end.

Walking into the house, I would think no one was here; it was just that quiet. I walked into Neron's study, and everyone was sitting around waiting. Nuru had her nose turned up, but I politely ignored her and took a seat in the only vacant chair, which was behind my husband's desk. If the bitch wants to be petty and mad, she can all the fuck she wants. I'll put her ass out with the quickness. This is still my shit after all.

Sitting in Neron's chair did something to me, and I could just feel his warmth. The smell of his expensive cologne lingered around and I'm probably crazy, but I could almost hear his voice calling to me.

"Mrs. Avery, if you don't mind, we are ready to start." Nero's lawyer spoke, and I nodded, allowing him to take the floor. He did the normal speech speaking about his businesses and who they were to be ran. When it was time to get to his assets and his estate, everyone perked up.

"I leave everything to my wife, Shantalya Rice-Avery."

I wish I could show you a picture. They were all plotting ways to kill me in their head. I politely rose from my seat and strutted my way out of the room. I heard Nuru ranting about contesting the will and making my life a living hell before a full wave of shouting started. They sounded like an angry mob.

I guess they ain't so fucking bougie when they realize their well is running dry. Neron told me one night that he takes care of all of his siblings including his mother. None of them are doing as well as they make it seems. They were depending on Neron's will to live off of, but Nuru really thought she was slick. She had one of his check-books and black cards so as long as he was still living, she could pull money from the account. The bitch really acted like she was so hurt that I pulled the plug, but she was really mad that I fucked up her pockets.

"Stay where you're at. I'm almost there. Ion trust how that shit just went down. They might be plotting on you since you big money banks now."

"Shut your ass up."

"Ok cool. I will if you do me a favor?"

"What you want, Tyrell?" I skeptically said because I know he about to play.

"Let me borrow a hunnid dollars. You got it."

"Boy bye and hurry up. I gotta meet Lai and Niyah at the spa in a minute."

"I'ight I'm coming up the street pull out now."

"So, it took Trouble locking yo ass up and slipping a baby in you for you to get a car and a cellphone. Bitch, had I know I would have hooked y'all up from the start," Niyah said from the backseat as Lai drove us to the spa. I really don't want to go, but I know she thinks this is what will make me feel better, so I'm coming with a smile on.

"Shut up, Niyah. Why couldn't that mouth go why the loud ass hair and other shit!" Lai spat, shocking the fuck out of the both of us.

"Bitchhhhhhhh! Let me find out Trouble got you putting some speck on yo name!" I had to laugh at Niyah this time cause she is running the fuck out.

"I guess Ice is still not fucking you, huh?"

"Bitch, no. We got so close the other night, but my phone went off from a text message, and he got mad cause I had a lock code on it. The nigga told me I lost my rights to have a lock on anything in his house. He told me I better not even lock my knees when I stand." Lai and I laughed so hard at that shit. Ice is turning it up some notches for this crazy heifer, and that's what her ass gets too.

"I really think these men all need counseling. Trouble is going, so maybe he can talk them into it too."

"Bitch, Trouble's in counseling?" Niyah took that shit right from my lips. I need her to say that shit again because clearly, I misheard.

"Yea, I told him to work on his issues, and he went to see a therapist." This bitch was saying the shit so plainly like she wasn't talking about sicking a wild animal on a damn therapist. Trouble gone drive them damn doctors slap crazy.

"Lai, do a group session and record it. I need you to do that shit for the culture. We all need to see this shit."

"No, I have my therapy, and he has his. I don't want to get into his past until he feels like telling me," she said as we parked outside a high-end spa.

We all got out heading inside. Niyah had to be extra and stunt in her tall heels, she toned it down some, but she will always and forever be extra and Ice gone have to just deal with all of it.

"Hello Welcome to Trinity Oasis, how may help you today?"

"Hey, I booked three vaginal steams and full body massages."

"Vaginal steams? Lai, you ain't say shit about that now!" Niyah snapped, making the receptionist turn bright red. Now her ass sees we are in an uppity ass place. Why is she cutting up.

"I will go and get the masseur," she said, hauling ass away towards the back.

"Niyah, just relax. We are here now, so let's just enjoy the shit" I reasoned, and she rolled her eyes.

"Umhumm next time you tell me when you volunteer my pussy for some shit." We didn't even bother responding to her crazy ass. We waited in silence until the masseur came out, and I knew by looking at the lady Niyah was about to be on some shit.

"Is this the woman who is doing the massages or the pussy streaming?" I hung my head in shame cause this bitch ain't have to run the fuck out like that.

"She will be assisting with both."

"Nah-uh, fuck that. I'mma need someone else, or I'm waiting in the fucking car."

"Ma'am we would be happy to assist you with that if you could just give me a reason for your request."

"How about because I don't want that bitch to fucking touch shit that's got to go up my pussy. It's a thousand and five degrees in this damn place, and she's got a whole bed quilt wrapped around her face. Ian racist but ion trust no fucking body whose face I can't see. That bitch might be about to shoot some anthrax up my pussy. I got a thousand fucking reasons, and all of them end with me not wanting her near me, Matter of fact I'm not sitting my pussy over not hot rocks and stream anyways. Lai and Shanty I'll be in the fucking car!" I felt so bad because I was laughing my ass off at Niyah, and I know this woman is feeling some type of way about that fucked up shit she said.

"Ma'am, I'm so sorry I will just pay for the session including the tip, and we will just leave. My friend didn't take her medication today, and she suffers from severe paranoid delusions. They had her locked up in a catholic asylum and the nuns were very harsh on her. Ma'am your hijab remind her of a nun's habit and she just zoned out. Please don't take any offense to her she didn't mean any harm,"

I lied my ass off, and the ladies nodded. Lai swiped her card, and I went ahead and swiped mine too. We had to at least pay this woman for her troubles cause Niyah just went too far with all that shit. Ice needs to hurry up and fuck her because her damn attitude is getting worse by the day.

"You ass is dead wrong for that shit!" I spat as we got into the car.

"No. Lai is wrong for trying me. She knows I don't play about my pussy ever since I had that bad wax. Blame her ass for bringing me out here. I'm already still sore from when Mama Rosemary came in and killed my last shot at getting some dick. I had Ice's ass primed and ready, and soon as I go to mount his ass, she busts through the door, beating the skin off my back with that damn back scratcher. I almost pissed on my damn self that shit hurt so damn bad. Fuck all this shit right now; I'm stressed the fuck out!"

"It wasn't about you Niyah. This was for Shanty to get her in a better mood, but you ruined that."

"She didn't, Lai. That bitch made my damn day telling that woman she was gone put anthrax up her pussy. I'm good so don't keep on worrying about me. It's one day at a time, and I'm going to cope with things slowly. I just love that you guys are here for me."

I pulled both of my bitches in for a hug, then told Lai to drop me off at Fame's house. I know I want to be with him, but we just have to take things extremely slow, especially until I come to grips with Neron's death. I just love the fact that Fame is being so patient and attentive. It's like I have the Fame I've been praying for my whole life. I just hope it lasts.

TWENTY-SEVEN

Trouble

Ian been back to that therapist bitch since she told me I needed to find my cracked-out birth moms. The bitch wanted me to do all the fucking talking and thinking while she just sits up there and listens adding her two cents in to make me feel like she was really helping. I could have Malaika listen to me in that case. Ian got time to be wasting no fucking money. The more I thought about the shit she said about talking to my birth moms the more sense that shit made. Lai thinks it's a good idea too, so that's what we're rocking with. I just want Lai back, so whatever she tells me I gotta do, I'm doing it.

I found the bitch that birthed me, upstate in a prison psychiatric facility. I worked it out with one of the guards so that he could put me on her visiting list. Ian got time for the bitch to decline my fucking visited. She's gone fucking see me and hear what I gotta say as well as give me some fucking answers.

Walking into the facility, my man handed me a pass, and we slapped hands before I headed back. I felt uneasy walking in, almost like I was nervous but that can't be it. I never sweat shit; I cause the sweating. Entering the huge day room, I spotted her immediately. She was sitting by a huge window on the window seat knitting something. Her hair was long and wavy down her back. She had a crotchet headband holding it back. I stood there silently admiring her beauty. Her dark skin glowed naturally, but the sunlight from the windows made her appear angelic. I was in awe of her, and for a moment I was that little nigga who loved the fuck outta his mama.

Like she felt me staring she turned her head and locked eyes with me. It was like a dream had come true with the amount of emotion and love that flooded through her eyes. Hopping up from the window, she dropped everything to rush over to me. Instinctively I caught her in my arms and held her tight.

"I prayed many nights that you would come around to look for me. I thank God you finally did," she said with tears distorting her soft voice. I just held her close feeling myself get worked up too. I thought I'd be mad seeing her, but all I feel is relief. Holding her in my arms makes this shit feel so fucking real. She pulled back, grabbing my hand to pull me towards the window and out the side door.

"Judy, is it okay for my son and me to sit out here and catch up?" A lady in the white gown nodded, and we took a seat at a circle table under a big tree.

"Don, you still look the same, boy. Every spit of my daddy, I know he's looking down proud of how big and strong you are. Just like I knew," she said with a smile. I just sat there staring at her. She looks so good that you would have never thought she was on drugs before.

"Why you so quiet, baby? Don't tell me you never grew out of that shyness?

"Nah, I grew outta that shit the first month of being in the system," I said it with unintended harshness, and it hit her hard.

"You had a hard time in there?"

"What do you think? You let me in a fucking store looking stupid. You ain't tell me shit nor did you prepare me for what shit was gone be like in there. Them nigga had a field day with my soft ass. They broke my arm before I finally grew the balls to stand up for myself."

"I never wanted that to happen, baby."

"What the fuck did you want to happen? You didn't give a fuck what happened cause if you did, you wouldn't have left me like that."

"That's what you think?"

"That's what the fuck I know." All of a sudden, she stood up reaching across the table and grabbed me by my ear to slap the shit out of the back go my head.

"Learn to watch your damn mouth when you're talking to me, boy. Ain't shit changed but my age; I will still fuck yo ass up. Sit upright, fix ya face, and listen to what I gotta say and hear me good!" I straightened my back and took the mug off my face. I remember her hands and her licks were just as powerful if not more than Mama Rosemary's. My mama used to get me in line with one look.

"I ain't proud of what I did by leaving you, but I know it was the best thing I could've done. Look where they got me at. My ass ain't crazy, but the shit I had done to Isaac's ass they had no other choice but to declare me insane. I messed around and killed Isaac trying to use his organ to create some more crack. I saw it on that damn TV show and thought I could do it too. That pipe had me going out my mind. I was doing any and everything for a hit.

Back when I still had you, I would be in that room Jonesing so bad it'll be telling me to get up and go sell you to somebody for more money. I knew then I had to get you away, I had the strength to fight them evil thoughts, but that damn Isaac would have done that to you. He brought the idea to my head in the first place. That's when I knew I had to get you out of there.

I picked that dollar store on the far end of town cause I knew that good worker would get you. She does right by the kids she gets. I planned everything all right for you. I wanted you to go to a family that could pay for you to play ball like you wanted. Don, I still say to this day that you were the best thing that ever happened to me and that ain't changed. I just got so caught up in a man that I let him drag me down to the gutta with him. I should have been a better mama to you. It's so much shit that could have been done differently, but everything works out in the ways that best fa us."

"So, you abandoned me to keep me away from you and that

nigga Isaac? Why do all that when you just could have got clean? You love me, but you left me to be raised by fucking strangers!" I barked, slamming my hands on the heavy wooden table as I stood to my feet.

I can't hear no more of this bullshit. This bitch is crazy for real if she thought that shit made fucking sense. She better hope I calm down or I'm sneaking back in this bitch and slitting her fucking throat. While I'm at it, I'm knocking that psychiatrist bitch out for suggesting this dumb shit.

"You won the national spelling bee that year and the next two in a row. You could have won the third year, but you misspelled marram, you replaced the last a with an e. I was watching you from a distance up until I killed Isaac. I kept good track of the man you were becoming. I may have made the wrong choices, but I did it all out of love. You might can't forgive me today, but someday when you can, come back and see about me sometimes."

I started walking backwards, rushing to get the hell out of there. I hopped in my ride and gripped my head shouting, trying not to let this shit fuck with my emotions. I should've never fucking came to see this bitch. She's trying to fuck with my mind.

"What do you want, Donavan?" Lai snapped, coming out of the bathroom wrapped in a towel. She just stared at me waiting for an answer as I stood in the middle of the room. She walked closer getting a look over harder.

"Is that blood! What the fuck did you do?" She yanked me towards the bathroom, and in my state, I willingly went. A nigga ain't got shit in him I'm just a body right now.

Pulling all my clothes off, she wrapped them in her towel and pulled me into the shower with her. She took her time and cleaned my body while humming to me the way she always does. Coming out of my little trance, I grabbed her face, looking her deep into her eyes.

"I love you, and I need you in my life. I can't think straight without you. Ion want shit to do with another bitch that ain't you—"

"Stop referring to me as that!"

"You gone trip on that bullshit or you gone let me tell you I love you for the first fucking time. Shit, now it's gone be the fucking last." She smiled hard pulling me towards her.

"There's my Trouble. You had me scared for a minute. I thought you had finally snapped all the way out."

I pulled her closer to me and held her kissing her soft lips as the hot water ran down my back. Lifting her up, I eased her down on my hard dick, and her pussy strangled my shit. I had to squeeze her thighs hard as fuck and let out a loud moan to keep from nutting.

"You're so fucking big," she moaned as I eased in and out of her. That pussy got wetter and wetter for me with each thrust. Her shit was wetter than the fucking water that was falling around us.

"Pop that pussy on this dick for me."

She started bouncing on my dick so fucking good that I leaned my back up against the wall and let her cut up on the dick. She must've missed the fuck out me like I missed her ass. Gripping her waist, I threw her up and down as she bounced on me. I was getting at her special spot trying to make her hit all the high notes.

"You like that shit?"

"Ohhhh, I love this dick! Just keep fucking me."

"Get down and bend over for me."

As soon as she put that pussy in the air, I took a knee and blessed her with daddy's long tongue. I licked her pussy so fucking good I had doing the cry baby on my shit. She was moving her sweet pussy up and down on my shit until I had her spraying harder than the shower head. Satisfied, I stood on my feet and filled her to the brim with dick. I had all ten inches in her tight pussy fucking her until it was talking to a nigga.

"Fuck Lai I'm about to nut."

She hit me with the death grip, sucking my shit dry as soon as I said that shit. I grabbed her waist to keep from falling over on her ass. I leaned up against the wall for a minute to catch my breath before we got out the shower and climbed in bed.

"Why were you covered in blood?"

I should have known she was going to start with all these fucking questions. It never fails that her ass asks a thousand and one questions after we fuck. I can fuck her ass to sleep she'll wake her special ass up to find some shit to wake me up and talk about.

"I went to see the mama of that bitch that killed herself and that bitch had some pictures of you posted up like she was plotting some shit. I was going there to make the bitch get ghost but seeing that sent me over, and I took my anger and shit out on her ass."

"Is everyone just out to kill me now?"

"Nah that other dead bitch's people are happy as fuck you killed her ass and they even happier that they cracked out son dead too. They cashed the fuck out on them deaths. Shit, you did them a favor, and they know it. You won't hear shit from them." She shook her head, and I knew it was because she wasn't happy with me calling the dead bitches out they name, but shit ion know they real names anyways.

"Why were you so angry?" she asked, changing the subject, and I took a deep breath.

"I went to see my birth mama today."

"How did that go?"

"She's full of shit, and I don't want to talk about that shit. I saw her, and that's all that fucking matter. I did that shit you suggested. Now we back together so that bullshit doesn't matter.

"Whatever, I'm going to bed. I'm too exhausted to deal with your attitude." I was happy as hell shit said that shit.

I pulled my phone out and hit Ice up about some shit before turning over and laying down with her ass. I ended up telling her everything that happened with my mama, and she started talking that Kumbaya shit and I made her shut the fuck up talking to me. Nobody is gone make me understand why that bitch left me in a dollar store. That was some fucked up shit, and I can't ever forgive her for that.

TWENTY-EIGHT

Ice

Ni gets on my fucking nerves, but at the end of the day, ian going no fucking where. I knew that the only way to get her ass to start acting with some sense was to stop giving her attention. She loves attention and dick more than anything, so I knew she would start acting with some common sense. The shit that I did with Trouble last night though might have her ass not fucking with me.

The nigga hit Fame and me up to come ride with him so that he can cool his head, but Fame was busy with Shanty. I wasn't doing shit at the time but trying watching the videos Rina had sent over. I was trying to get a pattern on that nigga Markus as to where he might have ran off to, but ian find nothing solid just yet. So, I rode out with Trouble, and I mentioned going to Ni's people house to rob they ass. I just wanted to fucking traumatized them like they did her by ripping lil dude from her arms.

Trouble keeps ski masks in his ride, and as soon as I mentioned the shit, we masked up and headed over. Shit, went left as soon as we got inside. Seeing them muh'fuckas sent me off, and I shot her pops in the stomach aiming for his intestines. I wanted that nigga to have to wear a shit bag, so he'll know ian for no shit when he thinks about coming near my fucking family. Yea I was high as fuck off some loud when I thought of that shit, but I stand by my choice.

I would've shot her ghetto ass mama too, but the bitch was so torn up about her husband that I knew that was enough to keep her in line. After that, we went to see about some shit that had to do with Lai and Trouble ended up going crazy on that bitch. We had to torch the house because I know that nigga left evidence because the scene was a fucking mess. Blood was everywhere, and the lady's body was sitting wide open like he was carving out her organs or some shit. I know I fucked up with her people, but the shit me and Trouble's planning gone make up for all that and then some.

"Ice, nigga, what the fuck y'all calling me out here for?" Fame asked, walking into my office down at the restaurant with Big Dee and Trouble coming in behind him.

"Trouble hit me about marrying Lai, and I'm on the same shit with Ni too. I already know this nigga is trying to marry mama, so are you trying to lock Shanty down or what?"

"Nigga, her husband just fucking died. Shanty's not gone fucking marry me. Ian even gone set myself up for failure by asking, but I can plan some other shit for her when y'all do y'all shit. What y'all trying to do?"

"I hit a travel agency up about a destination wedding we can make that shit a triple one. Ian letting Ni know about shit because her ass do too fucking much, and she'll have me spend a 100 mil on a wedding. Her ass is getting this deluxe wedding package and a life-time supply of dick."

"Bro, this is the Ice I missed. You were lame and boring when you were with Ali's dumb ass."

"Nigga, respect the dead!" I spat back, and he laughed harder.

"You killed the broad and you mad at me for being real?"

"I'm down with the joint wedding shit, but we gone have to step it up some cause Rosemary ain't having that bullshit, and ian got time to hear her mouth." Big Dee added.

"Nigga stop fronting; yo ass is scared of that back scratcher." We all laughed with Fame on that shit. Mama don't play with issuing out ass whooping when she gets mad.

"You damn right.'

"Lai doesn't require too much. She like simple shit." Trouble said leaning back on the couch.

"Yo, why the fuck y'all telling this shit to me like I'm the fucking wedding planner. Grabbing the brochure from my desk drawer, I tossed that shit to them niggas so they could get the planner's number. I just hope her ass gets so caught up in getting married that she doesn't even sweat me damn near killing her pops.

"Ice where are we going? I don't know if Anju has ever flown before or how he will react to it?" Ni fussed as she packed up our shit up.

"Ni, just chill and pack for the beach. Lil dude is old enough to handle riding on a plane; just relax." She looked at me for a while then smirked.

"You're up to something, and I'm going to find out what it is. You ain't been fucking with me now all of a sudden we back cool. Nah, ion trust this shit."

"Man, finishing packing this stuff so we can go. I planned a nice vacation for us so we can bond as a family." She gave me a skeptical look before slowly continuing to pack never taking her eyes off me. I eased my ass out the room because she was trying to make me uncomfortable to get me to talk. Ian telling her ass shit. I sat down in the family room with lil dude, and we watched cartoons.

"Anju, go up to your room."

I damn near wanted to glue his to the seat cause by the tone of her voice I knew some shit was up. Her ugly ass mama probably called her. As soon as lil dude hit the stairs, she was in my face pointing her long, pointy nail in the center of my fucking forehead.

"You got something you want to tell me?"

"Nah." I just said that to piss her off more for trying to bitch me. Ion care if I did shoot her cat eating ass daddy, she don't gotta point her finger all in my fucking face.

"So you and Gip didn't rob my fucking parent's house while you shot him! He had to go through two surgeries, and he's still touch and go!" she shouted, and I just shrugged.

"That's fucked up that somebody did that to your pops, but it wasn't me." As soon as I said that shit, she hauled off slapping the shit out of my ass, scratching my face with her sharp as nails in the process. That shit felt like a wild cat clawed my ass. Grabbing my cheek, I hopped up, knocking her to the ground.

"Keep your fucking hands off me before I beat your fucking ass!" I gritted. I wasn't trying to raise my voice and have lil dude get the impression I'm beating on his mama.

"You can cancel all them fucking plans. I'm not going anywhere with your stupid ass. You better hope I don't go get my bedazzled .9 mil and come shoot you in your fucking neck. Ion give a fuck what happened between me and them that's still my fucking father! I'm the one that can make the choice to cause them pain, not you!"

I felt bad that she was sitting there crying, but ion care one bit about shooting her daddy. I'll do that shit all over again too. It ain't like the nigga dead any fucking ways. Her mama's lucky ian spiteful or I'll go shoot her for calling and snitching. She ain't never called Ni about shit, but she hurried up and called to snitch about that shit.

"I planned our wedding so you gotta come, Ni." Ion care if it looks like a bitch for begging, but I am.

"Nigga are you fucking retarded? I'm not fucking marrying you! I barely want to be near yo dumb ass right now, so do you really think..." she started going off on me in Korean. She was flaming my ass up, and all I could do was stand there and take her point her finger in my face.

"It's not just our wedding though. Trouble is marrying Lai, and Big Dee is marrying Mama Rosemary. I already spent the fucking money planning this shit for you."

"You must think I'm booboo the damn fool! You planned that thrown together ass wedding thinking that it was gone get me, but you got me fucked up. Ain't nobody falling for your stupid ass shit. Book me and Anju another room cause I'm not sleeping next to your stupid ass and don't fucking grabbed my ass when I walk away."

As soon as she passed, I grabbed a hand full of her juicy ass, and she turned around and punched me in the chest. I know she said don't grab her ass, but that just some shit I do on instinct. Every time I see her walking away, I gotta grab a handful. I guess I can cancel our ceremony cause I know I can't talk her into that shit. I'mma have to go ahead and drop some bands and plan her some shit that I know will get me back in her good graces. Right now, I'm just happy she ain't leave me for that shit.

"So Troub and Lai are the only two getting married tomorrow?" Fame asked, laughing at our asses.

"Man Rosemary cussed me out as soon as we got in the hotel room today. How the fuck did she even know, we were planning this shit?"

"Man, mama is a fucking KGB sleeper. She's got a chip embedded in her brain, and the satellites feed her information and shit."

"Real shit?" me and Trouble stop to just stared at Big Dee. Ain't no way this nigga believing that shit Fame talking.

"That nigga is feeding you with a kiddie spoon," Trouble said making us laugh.

"You can't listen to this nigga when he starts smoking. He'll have you believing in aliens and shit," I added.

"Nigga y'all tripping but that shit is real. The government got an army of aliens, bruh. They train them to look and act like regular people and do all the shit we do so that they can influence people's minds."

"Trouble, take that blunt out bro's hands. He's too far past his limit right now." Trouble flicked the blunt from Fame's hands, and he was so high that he didn't even protest.

"Man, I'm so nervous about this shit. I got everything planned just right for her. It's not too plain, but it's not all that fancy and over the top. It's some shit that she would be happy about, but what if she says no."

"Bro, You just told her you love her for the first fucking time three day ago. I guarantee she's not saying no to you finally opening up and showing her ass you really care about her. Shit, I'm proud to see that you actually put in an effort to plan some shit out for her cause I just signed Ni up for the deluxe package and put the money up for the shit."

"And that's why you're sitting here looking like you got caught by a wild cheetah." Fame let in making me get tight.

"Yo Fame fuck you bro," he fell out laughing and I waved his ass off as usual.

"Aye, bro! You getting married tomorrow, so we gotta give you a bachelor party nigga." Fame said, standing on his feet grabbing his phone.

"Siri, direct me to where the hoes are at in Antigua." We fell out laughing when Siri gave this nigga directions to a fucking bar. Shit, Siri got all the answers, so we followed the directions to the bar and celebrated my bro's last night being a free man. Sis accomplished a great task by locking this nigga down.

TWENTY-NINE

Lai

"LAIIIIII!" Niyah loud voice echoed throughout the room, sounding like an annoying siren. I flipped over tossing the pillow at her to shut her the fuck up. I had heartburn so bad last night that it kept me up tossing and turning plus Trouble never came in, so there's no telling what he got into.

"What do you want, Niyah?"

"Come on and get up, Malaika. It's a pretty ass day out on this big beautiful island, and I know you want to go look around. We have a whole spa day set up minus that pussy steaming shit. We got a girl coming to do our hair and makeup because Trouble's planned something special for you," Niyah said with Shanty beside her nodding in agreement.

"No, I don't feel well, and if Donavan Troy has planned something for me you two go tell him to get his ass in here and tell me himself. I'm not putting up with any of his shit no more. He stayed out all night while I was tossing and turning suffering from heartburn. You tell him I said I"M NOT DOING SHIT!" I hissed, and they stared at me with shocked expressions.

"Baby Trouble done put some fire off in you. Don't let me find out my niece gone be a baddie." Shanty laughed, but I didn't find anything funny.

"I told your ass we should've come in here with Mama Rosemary!" I heard Niyah snap as they walked out. I politely laid back down pulling the covers over my head. I was peacefully sleeping when he came in standing over me. I felt his presence and jumped up looking around.

"Get up and go with Shanty, mama, and Ni. I got some shit planned for you later, and I want you to be right for it."

"Where were you last night?"

"I was kicking it with my niggas," he said it like it was just nothing for him to stay out all damn night.

"Well, I'm kicking it with myself today. Leave me alone, goodbye." I laid back down and before I could pull the covers up he yanked me to my feet. I immediately scrunched my body up protecting my stomach screaming, "I'm pregnant!"

"I'm not about to lay hands on you. Stand up straight so I can do this shit right." I looked at him cautiously, as I stood upright. He took a deep breath and got down on one knee grabbing my left hand. I got so nervous that I started to get itchy. I know he is not about to propose to me, my mind is playing tricks on me. Maybe he has to tie his shoe or something, but he cannot be about to propose.

"Ion know how to do this shit or how it's supposed to go. All I know is that I need you in my life and nothing or nobody is coming in between us. I'll spend the rest of my life doing whatever makes you happy and protecting you and our child with everything in me. Will you marry me?"

Tears were rolling down my face as I nodded yes frantically. He picked me up, hugging me tightly in his arm. The door opened, and everyone else pilled in.

"Now can we go and get pampered?" Shanty asks.

"Yes, let's go get pampered."

He put me down, and I took a quick shower, slipping on a pink maxi dress and thong sandals, and I headed out to prepare for my wedding. I don't really care how fancy the ceremony is just as long as he says I do everything else is fine with me. I was in a daze the whole day as we went through the different processes. From the massage and facials all the way to the mani and pedis. I would have still been on cloud nine if Niyah hadn't brought me back down to force me into deciding between dresses.

There was a short halter neck one and a long off the shoulder flowy one with slits up the sides to show small peeps of my legs. I like the long one better because it would accent small baby bump. The girls all seemed pleased by my choice too. After that, I started being pulled in a million directions. Everything was happening so damn fast that I started to get a little light headed. I had to take a seat to get my head together. As I was sitting someone knocked on the suite door and Shanty rushed over to get it. It was room service. The man rolled a big tray of food, and as soon as he uncovered it, my stomach growled. It was a big juicy steak with a baked potato;

"Mr. Troy left specific instructing for me to check your steak to ensure that it was fully cooked. He had concerns about it being undercooked and harming the baby." After he cut the steak making sure it was well done he left with Mama Rosemary tipping him.

"I just want to know how that conversation went though," Niyah said as I tore into the food. It was so fucking good, and if I didn't love that man before, I sure love his ass now.

"Aye, bitch, let me order that number three on the menu," Shanty said, mimicking Trouble.

"Yea and that shit better be done cause my bitch is pregnant and ion want shit happening to my baby," Niyah added.

"Let me see any pink, and I'm painting these walls with all y'all blood. Ion fuck around about mine." Shanty said, and I couldn't help but laugh at them because that is probably verbatim how that conversation went.

"Leave my baby alone. He's getting better."

"That he really is. I never thought I'd see the day that my meanest son would settle down. Ion mean to get the mood all sad, but Malaika, I just gotta tell you how thankful I am that you came into Trouble's life. I know the problems you faced with him and for you to stick around lets me know that you are a strong woman. He's going to push and be stubborn, and you gotta push back. Show him that you mean business, and he'll get in line. I just want to welcome you into this crazy family." I stood to my feet with my plate and hugged her tight.

"Girl! Your greedy ass could have put that plate down," Niyah said, causing us all to laugh. We enjoyed the rest of the day getting prepped for my ceremony, and I had to constantly remind myself to remain calm because my nerves we all over the place.

"You look soooo pretty!" Shanty said, hugging me.

My makeup was done subtly perfect. It gave me such a natural glow like I just woke up sun-kissed. My hair was in its naturally curly state with I had a flower veil adorning my head like a tiara. I felt so beautiful as we walked through the path to get to the private beach. My heart nearly stopped when I spotted my father standing at the end of the path.

"You look heavenly, angel" I ran into his arms, and he hugged me back. "Your mother is in the front row waiting."

"How did you know?"

"Donavan and I have been associates for years, now. I never knew you two were an item, but as I have said to him, I couldn't pick a better man. He will hold you dear and protect you, and that's all any father could ask for."

"I know y'all having a special moment, but bro is losing his mind thinking Lai is standing him up. We gone need to get this shit on the road or he might fuck around and drown the pastor," Fame said, and with that we got things started.

"Giving Myself Over" by Jenifer Hudson started playing faintly in the distance as my father step up to me caressing my cheek softly, making me feel like I was his little angel for the first time in many years.

"There was a time I thought I never get to do this. Having this moment with you means the world to me. Angel, I promise to be a better father and grandfather." A tear slipped down as I locked my arm in his.

"I know that you will." With that, he guided me down the aisle.

The colors for our wedding were coral and teal. The bright flowers were lining the deck that led out across the clear waters. It was so small and elegant, simply perfect for me. Only the necessary people are here to see this magical moment. My eyes landed on Trouble and my heart skipped a beat. He looked so good in his tailored tan suit. His chocolate skin looked deeper with the added contrast of his tan suit and coral shirt.

We made it to the end of the alter, and my daddy gave over to him as he pulled me close just staring into my eyes with tears welling in his. The amount of love that I saw staring back was everything my heart and soul ever needed. From that look alone, I would give him my entire heart. I will be his equal in every single way, upholding him as my king for the rest of my life.

~

Trouble and I have been back from Antigua for a few days. It feels so amazing to be married. After all he and I have been through it feels surreal to finally get our happy ending. I almost wanted to extend our honeymoon for another week, but the way my pregnant body is set up Trouble would have had me on strict bed rest. My pussy has never been used so much in all of my life. He literally woke up and fell asleep inside of me. I am tired, and I'm just happy that he has something to do with his brothers all day because if not, he'd be up in there now.

I flopped back down on the couch, writing music in my notebook. Lately, I've been contemplating writing an uplifting album. Just something that people can listen to start to finish and be positively influenced. From my time volunteering, I've seen what music can do and I just have strong faith that will have a huge impact on the world. Something lit up and buzzed on the table catching my attention. Looking down, I saw that it was Trouble's phone. Shaking my head, I let out a light laugh knowing that his mind is still on our honeymoon. We were so wrapped up in one another that we just left our phone sitting on the coffee table. Picking it up, I grew hot with anger looking at the message.

Maybe: Debbie - It's been a little minute and this kitty been missing you. <Video attachment>

I immediately clicked out of the video of her playing in her dirty vagina tossing his phone aside. Now, I'm pissed that I never really confronted him about sleeping with her the first time. I'm not stupid enough to believe it was just once. I was dumb then, but I'm not playing the stupid role no fucking more. I'm about to make how I feel about the situation crystal clear. I'm hand delivering him a message that I know he'll understand. I grabbed my phone calling Shanty and Niyah telling them to get ready to do a pull-up. This type of shit is the only thing his ass responds to anyways. They got me fucked up though. I am Mrs. Troy now, and this little side bitch shit is something I refuse to tolerate.

THIRTY

Markus

They thought they had the one up on me, but I'm always a step ahead. I swapped Archie's phone out with one with a mic several weeks back and ever since I had been listening to his every move. I knew that he had potential, but I never make the mistake of trusting a man who was willing to give up his homie. If he'd turn on him, then I know for a fact he'd flip on me down the line. He was just means to an end anyways.

He wouldn't have lived to see the next day after Ice and Fame were dead. Ice saved me the trouble by offing him. I was sitting in my office watching the live feed like I do overnight after our meetings. Something just old me to listen to the feed from Archie's cell. I heard that whole bitch ass speech Ice gave and everything. He's still wet behind the ears in towards a lot of shit in the game. Niggas ain't shit, and there is no loyalty in the street life. Money and power will turn the purest heart black.

Since that night, I've been staying with Debbie, a little broad I've been fucking for years. She was a teenager when we first started messing around twenty years ago. I must say after twenty years her pussy still nice and tight. The pussy is amazing, but that's not the reason I'm laying low at her house. She runs a gambling ring in her living room, and I need to be around to hear the word on the streets. Plus, I know Debbie's been fucking around with Trouble for some years, and I'm trying to bait Rosemary's address out of her. If I get that address, then my plans are back in motion.

With them being down with The Camp my resources are limited, and I don't know who I can trust. My reach is wide, but The Camp's reach could extend to outer space. Shit, their sister found out shit from my past when most of the people I ran with dead and gone. They got connections everywhere, and I can't risk running into somebody who down with them. So, I'm rocking off the radar by myself. I plan to call them once I'm inside Rosemary's house to make them all rush over. Then I'm blowing the entire house. I want them all gone, including Trouble. Killing Rosemary will cause him to be on my trail, and I don't have time for that shit.

"What are you thinking about, daddy" Debbie purred, climbing into my lap. I grabbed her by her ass pulling her up to me.

"How sweet and tight that pussy is." I pulled her small shorts to the side and eased up into her, giving her deep grinding thrust as her walls held me firmly.

"Markus! Ohhh shit! Fuck me good, baby!"

Leaning forward, I used my teeth to free her juicy breasts from her top and took one into my mouth. Swirling my tongue around, I gently sucked it, making her pussy flood me with her cum. Using her hot spot to my advantage, I flicked my tongue on her hardened nipple back and forth as her pussy thumped around my dick.

"You like that shit, huh?"

"Ooohhhh yes, bite down on it."

I gently clamped my teeth on her nipple, causing her to grip my back with her nails. That turned me on, and I flipped her over to take her over the top. Grabbing her inner thighs, I spread her legs wide and fucked her tight pussy until it was emptying cum all over me. She had my dick creamy and soaking wet with her juices. She was on number three, but I was just getting started. Flipping her over, I ran my dick up and down her wet slit then went deep into her ass.

"FUCK!" I groaned as I breeched her opening. Grabbing a

hand full of her hair, I eased in and out stretching her slowly. Once she had accepted me, I sped up my pace, snaking my finger around to strum her clit.

"AHHHH!" she moaned as I fucked her ass.

"Fuck I'm about to nut. Where you want it?"

Like the good freak she is, she moved off my dick turning around to swallowed it whole. She sucked the nut straight out of me, and we both collapse down on the bed with me pulling her close, getting ready to butter her ass up.

"You love me?" I asked, causing her to look at me with a smile. After all this dick I stuffed in her ass she better fucking love a nigga.

"Of course, I do. I'm just waiting for you to finally leave your wife."

"Why you think I'm here now? I'm not going back to her it's you and me forever. I just need to handle one thing, and we can disappear together and live happily." Her smile grew so huge that I knew she'd do whatever just to be with me. "I just need one small thing from you." I gently rubbed her back, kissing her on the neck as I spoke.

"Anything."

"What's Rosemary's address?" My question caused her to stiffen. I know she was contemplating the risks of not telling, so I rushed to smooth it over better.

"They're trying to kill me to take over my operations. It's them or me, and I need our help so we can be happy together, baby. Twenty years is a long wait, and I'm ready to make it official. I'm trying to marry you."

"Really?" she beamed, and I licked my lips with a quick head nod.

She reached over, grabbing the notepad and pen from the bedside dresser and wrote down the address I was smiling ear to ear knowing that I was finally bout to get rid of those pieces of shit. Debbie doesn't know how much she just saved me, and after this, I may just run away with her. Shit she's been holding me down this damn long why not go all in.

Creeping through the front door that was surprisingly unlock, I made my way inside. It was dark in the entrance way, but I could see a light flickering off the wall, signaling that a TV was on. Stalking towards the living room, I immediately looked up and the TV screen that had words flashing across.

"GOTCHA!!" Before I could react, I was riddle with bullets and the lights popped on.

"Yo, what the fuck? I thought we were waiting to get answers first!" Ice barked, standing over my body kicking my gun away.

"Nigga that's you on that Curious George shit. Don't nobody else give a fuck what that nigga gotta say," Fame retorted.

"Well, you got a couple of minutes before that nigga finally kicks the bucket. Ask what the fuck you wanna know," Trouble said with a shrug of his shoulders.

Feeling weaker by the second, I managed to pull myself up against the wall. I could feel my heart thumping wildly, and it became harder and harder to breathe as blood filled my lungs. I know that this is my last stand, so I'm going out with a fucking bang.

"You want answers, punk ass nigga!" I spat weakly with blood spewing from my mouth.

"Nigga, say yea so we can gone kill this motherfucker! Ian got time for this shit!" Fame spat impatiently.

I had to laugh at him because none of us were making it out of this motherfucker. I laughed too hard and began to cough violently spewing blood and chunks of my organs with each cough. My chest felt heavier and heavier each time.

"Aye, gone say what the fuck you gone say for real."

"I compromised my soul for this shit. The minute I raped that innocent girl, I was tainted and it wasn't no coming back from that. If my soul was the price I had to pay, I was taken over this shit and having it all for myself. I poisoned my father to take over the throne, but he played me with that bullshit clause in his will. He wanted this shit to carry on for generations to come. He had hopes of his legacy carrying on forever, but I had other plans. I wanted this shit all for me and when I died, I made sure it was leaving with me. I worked too hard for any other nigga to reap the benefits of what I corrupted myself for!" I spat with the last bit of my strength.

"This motherfucker is retarded. We don't want no part of a fucking prostitution and sex trafficking ring. Nigga, that shit was all yours, anyways. Ice, I'm about to gone kill this nigga cause he talking stupid."

Just as Fame said that, I heard the front door open and soon after the woman found their way to us all. Their eyes grew wide looking at my body riddled with bullet wounds. They just didn't know that they had just gave a dying man great satisfaction. My legacy will die with me and I get to take all these fuckers and their bitches out to.

"WHAT A FUCKING WAY TO GO!" I laughed sinisterly lifting the detonator. They may have caught me slipping, but they never stopped me from planting the bomb at the back of the house. I took my last breath with a feeling a pure bliss taking over me. Markus for the fucking win! I pressed the detonator as the life slipped from my body. I'll see them all in hell.

THE END (or nahhh)

Epilogue (Four years later)

Niyah & Ice

AYEEEEEE! I'm up first, bihhhhhhhh! I know damn well y'all didn't believe we died. I got too much to live for to ever go out like that. That nigga was so focused on planting the bomb he didn't realize that Gip and Big Dee were standing back there watching him the whole time. Gip's G.I. Joe ass disabled the bomb, carried it right on over to Markus's mansion, and blew all his shit up. I just wish he would have lived long enough to see that the damn bomb never went off.

I would have paid to see his reaction to that shit or even to have him hear how we stood out in the hallway of Debbie's house listening to him ask her for Mama Rosemary's address. We texted our men as soon as we heard that shit. To be a police officer the nigga was extremely careless cause when he got up to leave the house. Lai, Shanty, and my ass were hiding behind the curtains. That nigga just scrolled on by like he didn't see a thing.

As soon as he left, Lai went right into the room and gave Debbie's old ass three head shots, and we left her house headed straight to Mama Rosemary's to watch shit play out. To be real when Lai called us to tell us she was about to go kill Debbie, I thought that bitch was lying. Shit, I told her I was down because I knew she wasn't gone do it, but that little bitch fooled the hell out of me. Trouble must have gave her some act right on that honeymoon because she killed that bitch and walked out cheesing hard as hell, but enough about the past. They are both dead and that's all the fuck that matters.

I stayed mad at Ice for shooting my daddy for a few months, but he dropped half a mil on our wedding and that made a bitch feel way better. I wasn't really too mad he shot my evil ass daddy anyways because I contemplated killing him many nights. I was just mad that he made that choice without consulting me first. I was in heat for him after that long as sex break too cause I got pregnant on my wedding night. Now, we have a two and a half old son, Ignacio Jr. Ice has been trying hard to knock me up again, but I'm not going for that shit. We don't have time for another baby righ tnow.

I just opened two more nail shops and three dance studios where I do pole dance lessons and fitness classes. On top of that Ice's businesses have been booming too, and he's been working on opening restaurants out of state and internationally in the future. Our fingers are crossed for the overseas ones. My baby works so damn hard y'all, and I'm there with him every step of the way. We on our Jay Z and Beyoncé shit. What's better than one billionaire? TWO!

"Mom, dad and Lil Ice are making a mess in the kitchen and I just want to say I had no parts in it," Anju snitched, causing me to laugh.

Ice is always finding crazy shit to do in order to bond with the boys. Anju is only snitching because they broke a damn window last week, and I took his cell phone. Any other time his ass would be right down there fucking shit up with them. Walking into the kitchen, they had flour, frosting, and dirty pots everywhere.

"Ignacio, what the fuck?" He just looked up at me with a smile and shrug of his shoulders.

"I'm teaching my sons that men can bake cakes too. Just roll with me on this, Ni."

"Hell no. Jr. get down and go wash up. Anju help him get

cleaned up." As soon as they left, I was ready to light into his ass, but he swooped me up sitting me on the messy counter.

"Stop all that fussing and let me get in them guts. I think we need a little diva, next." I was getting ready to cuss him out until he starting sucking and licking on my spot.

"OOOOH! You can have as many as you want" My horniness was talking for me as his hands traveled down finding their way into my panties.

"Yea, that's what I thought. I'm about to murder this pussy, Ni."

Ok, y'all have had enough of my sex life with my man. We're married now so this shit we about to do is sacred and just for me and him. Just know that everything is all good in the Esperilla household.

Shanty & Fame

"Oh, my God! Are we really doing this?"

"Hell yeah! You had that fairy tale shit, now let's do some shit that you will never forget."

Laughing at him, I laced my hands in his as we walked towards the plane. I don't know how, but I let him talk me into getting married t in the air before we jump out of a damn plane. Fame is so damn off the charts, but like he said this will be a moment that I will never forget. I know he's doing it to top my wedding with Neron, even though I've told him a million times our love is different.

Like Neron said in his death letter, our love was necessary for my growth, but we were never meant to be. My heart has belonged to Fame since I was a little damn girl. I just needed him to get his shit together, and I can finally say that he has. It took four years of him proving himself to me for me to accept his proposal. Every year he proposes, praying that I will say yes and this time I did. I'm finally ready to marry the man that I know I'm going to spend forever with and forget about the rest of the bullshit.

Speaking of bullshit, I finally got that sad and bougie bitch off my back. After years of her going to the courts trying to contest Neron's will, she finally got the picture and stopped fucking with me.

Well, quiet as kept Fame went to her house and killed her boyfriend in front of her face and she politely boarded a plane to her private island the next day. I haven't heard a peep from her old miserable ass ever since. Neron's business is thriving and all his profits go to charity and technological research. That's what Neron would have wanted, and I made it my mission to honor that. It's the least I can do.

"Aye, stop thinking about that nigga when you about to marry me!" Fame spat, causing me to laugh. He knows me too damn well and sometimes I can't stand it.

"So, you jealous?"

"You damn right. You gone make me go blow his family tomb up." I smacked him on his chest laughing so hard tears fell. He pulled me close to him, kissing my lips softly.

"You remember that day I crept into your hospital room?"

"Yea, what about it?'

_"I told you then that I was gone be the nigga you end up with when I story ends, didn't I?"

"Yea, you did, and I thought your ass was fucking crazy. I didn't want shit to do with you after you fucked up my wedding, but you knew I could never stay away— at least not for long."

"That's cause you was made for a nigga like me. But seriously, you ready to do this shit, with me?" I nodded my head yes and he picked me up spinning me around in the air.

"Let's go take this fucking dive into our future, baby!" he shouted, titling his head back causing his loud voice to carry off in the distance.

"Let's go," I said giving him a quick peck still in his arms. A while later we were saying I do and jumping off the plane hand in hand, diving into the rest of our lives together— LITERALLY!

Trouble & Malaika

I walked through the warehouse laying niggas down without hesitation. Shit seemed like some action movie shit the way niggas just keep swarming out. Ducking behind a wooden crate, I reloaded both my guns and stood back up laying the remaining niggas down. Once all the men were dead, I rushed over to the table in the center of the floor grabbing the large suitcase.

Curious to what the fuck the nigga had me stealing that was worth all this fucking trouble, I popped the bitch open and it was a sparkling necklace with rubies lining it. The shit was so fucking beautiful the way it sparkled under the dim lights. I knew this shit had to be priceless. This some shit that the Egyptians were buried in, I'm sure of it.

"I'll take that," the nigga who hired me spoke, causing me to look back.

He was standing there with a bad ass exotic bitch beside him. The bitch had her .9 mil pointed at me like she was nasty with that shit. I chuckled, realizing they played me. The nigga told me I was collecting something that was rightfully his when he was really sitting my ass up for a jewel heist.

"The only way I'm handing shit over is if you snatch it from my dead body."

"That can be arranged, Anna." He said pointing to the exotic bitch. She smirked, wrapping her finger around the trigger, but before she could fire, bullets went flying knocking their domes off.

"I thought we agreed that we weren't taking any more jobs until our prince arrives?" Lai spat. I turned around and pulled her sexy ass to me rubbing her swollen belly. I turned my bitch into my fucking partner, and we going hard in these streets.

"Nah, I said you wasn't taking anymore. I'm always working to feed my family."

"Unhmm, you almost got your ass killed. That's what happens when Mr. Troy leaves home without the Mrs. I'm so happy this happened too, now you see why you need me. I've been declining this job for months because I knew he was up to something," she fussed.

"True, but at least I got you something pretty to rock later when I'm up in them guts."

"And what's that?" she said with huge smile. I turned opening the suitcase again and her eyes sparkled, looking at the necklace. She stared at it for a while before putting on her tough face again.

"I guess that makes up for it, but you're still in deep shit. Why must you always get into these situations?"

"Cause my name is Trouble! I wouldn't be me if I didn't stir shit up every now and then."

"Yea grab the suitcase and let's go. We have to go to our daughter's dance recital in the morning and, we have plans with my parents in the afternoon."

So, the queen requests it is done. I grabbed the suitcase and followed her out. Shit, our marriage is better than ever and a nigga couldn't ask for nothing better. We got our 3-year-old daughter with my little boy on the way plus her parents are in her life heavy, now. Everything has worked out better than I ever expected. I even go up to visit my mom for time to time. Just to let her know that I forgive her and don't hold no hard feelings.

Lai giving birth to our daughter, Malai, helped me to understand what my moms meant by what she did. It wasn't the best choice, but it was a sacrifice she made with a better future for me in mind. Now, I just do all I can to build up for lost time and Lai even goes up to see her with Malai every other weekend. Our daughter loves her grandparents with all her heart and it lets me know that we made the right choice in forgiving our parents. Shit is one hunnid in our world, it's Trouble & Malaika Forever!

The Real End :)

MORE BY SHAYE B.

EVERY GANGSTA NEEDS A RIDAH
TROUBLE & MALAIKA: NOT YOUR AVERAGE LOVE STORY
EVERY GANGSTA NEEDS A RIDAH 2
TROUBLE & MALAIKA 2
HEAVY IS THE HEAD THAT WEARS THE CROWN
(**COMING SOON**)

CPSIA information can be obtained
at www.ICGtesting.com
Printed in the USA
LVOW10s2339190118
563260LV00021B/865/P

9 781983 480256